PARADISE & CHAOS

TOY

Paradise & Chaos

CHAPTER 1

Paradise

The one thing I hated was being late, that's exactly what I was right now. It wasn't totally my fault though but, still. Running around my room I was steady laying my own ass out. I knew I shouldn't have gone out for drinks after the photo shoot last night. Instead of going with my first thought I took my grown as out with Mecca and her assistant. Mecca was this up and coming fashion designer that lived in Hampton. She started out making clothes for her homegirls at a discounted price while she was still in high school. That was almost nine years ago. In that time span Mecca was now one of the most sought after designers for every one in the seven cities. She wasn't just making regular everyday outfits, homegirl was making gowns, baby clothes, she had even designed some of the cheerleader uniforms for a couple of the high schools in the area. She was doing the damn thing.

I met her after her third year of designing. One of her friends had recommended me to do one of her clients makeup that was running behind schedule for an event. I beat her clients face to the gods and the rest is history. I was now the only makeup artist that she used for any of her clients that didn't have one already. Last night she held her annual fashion show so of course I had to be there. My day had started at four thirty and didn't end until I opened my door at three this morning. I had fun with them but, I was paying for it dearly right now. I knew yesterday was going to be a long day so today was my planned self care day. I had booked an appointment at one of the local black owned spa named Natural Elements Spa and Salon. I even purposely made the appointment later in the afternoon so I wouldn't be late. That didn't do no damn good my appointment was at three o'clock and it was two thirty according to the clock on the dresser. By the time I put my clothes on and drove the twenty minutes it took for me to get to Chesapeake, if there wasn't any traffic I would be cutting it close. I couldn't even decide what I was going to wear so I could leave the house. Finally, I sat on the bed to search for my cell phone that was buried under the clothes that I had thrown on the bed while looking for something to put on. Once I found it I called the spa and rescheduled my appointment for another day. Since I did that I could now relax and take a breath. My phone rang and of course it was my sister Ivy. Ivy was the total opposite of everything that I was. She was more disciplined as my parents would say. She had control of everything in her life. Well, she did before her and Toxin got together. Even with him distracting her from being a control maniac she still kept things in order.

"Hey sis what are you doing today?" I answered.

"Nothing, I was calling to see how the fashion show went yesterday," she told me.

"Long, tiring but worth every minute of it. I even went out for drinks after with Mecca and her assistant," I told her.

"I like Mecca she has a good head on her shoulders. Even with her blowing up she hasn't changed from what I can tell. She's a good person to have in your circle sis. Speaking of your circle how are the ratchet rejects doing?" She asked.

I rolled my eyes because Ivy has never liked the two chics that I hang out with. She always told me to watch them or how they weren't really my friends. Yeah, they had some ways that caused me to give them a side eye but, they haven't crossed me that I know of yet. We had all known each other since middle school and even back then Ivy didn't like them.

"Porscha just bought a new car. I haven't seen it yet though. Angie her regular self, not doing nothing but, running behind her no good man," I said.

"Did either of them call to wish you good luck yesterday? I know they didn't come because Mecca was gonna have to put their asses out like she did the last time," Ivy said.

"No, I haven't heard from either of them in a few days. How's Toxin and my nephew doing?" I asked while rolling my eyes.

"Don't try to change the subject on me heifer. I'm not gonna say nothing else about your nothing ass friends. They're both fine SJ is playing basketball so he keeps us on the go. Life is good over here lil' sister," she said laughing.

"You stay flaunting those measly two years in my face. It ain't my fault mama and daddy didn't get it right the first time so they had to make me," I told her laughing.

We always went back and forth with each other about our ages. It wasn't like she was five years older than me but, she sure acted like it most of the time. Those two years meant nothing to me sometimes you would think that I was the older one.

"You wish that was the reason. You sound tired. If you don't have anything to do then go to bed and chill for the rest of the day. You deserve a break. I keep telling you that you're working yourself to death. I remember when I was the workaholic in the family. Get out and get some fresh air if you don't go to sleep. Just go with the flow today," she advised me.

"Who are you and what did you do to my sister? I know damn well this ain't Ivy Dixin on the other end of this phone. I remember when you worked around the clock even on holidays you were going in the office working ten hours days and shit. Let me find out Toxin has that change your thought process type of dick," I laughed.

"Don't put this all on him. Growth brings about change in everything around and in you," she said making me laugh even harder.

"You're my sister and I love you dearly. We all know that Toxin is the one that brought about this change. If you want to keep it spiritual and all, do you boo. I don't feel like staying in the bed all day so I'll find something to do. No worries I'm not gonna call you to see if you can come be with the single sister," I told her.

"Good then we ain't gonna have to argue about it," Toxin said clear as day.

"Oh bitch I know you ain't have me on speaker phone while you touching and feeling all on him. Y'all need to stop being so damn nasty all the time," I said hanging up on both of them.

I know I gave them a hard time but, I loved what they have. He made my sister happy and took her out of her old person ways. Before he came along it was a battle for me to get her to do anything besides working and more working. Now, she was more relaxed and smiled more. My uptight sister had found her happiness and that made me happy. Before I knew it my phone was ringing again. I picked it up thinking that it was my sister but got the shock of a lifetime.

"Yes, I clicked you off you know I don't do speaker phones and shit," I said laughing.

"Who the fuck you just banged on? I know it better not be another nigga. You keep testing me and I'm gonna have to show out watch what I tell you," Martrell fussed.

"Why are you calling me?" I asked rolling my eyes and taking a long, loud, exaggerated sigh.

"I'm calling you because I miss you and I love you. Who was you just talking to?" He asked.

"Do you pay my phone bill? Did you have sex with my mama to get her pregnant with me? I don't have a regular nine to five so I know you're not my supervisor," I said.

"What does any of that have to do with what I asked you?" He asked.

"Being that the answer is NO for everything I just asked you I ain't telling you shit. If you think it was just another nigga on my phone then yup that's who it was. I'm not answering because you're not my daddy, you don't pay my phone bill, and I work for myself so the only person I have to answer to is god," I told him.

"You always have some smart shit to say. We belong together. You shouldn't let these hoes out here breakup that good shit that we had," His ignorant ass said.

Martrell was my on and; off man. He had a serious dick problem. The problem was he couldn't stop fucking other women with it. His cheating was the reason we were more off than being together. He took the term 'fight for your relationship' to an entirely unheard-of level. Every time I turned around there was some chic telling me that she was calling to tell me about 'OUR' man. The first couple of times I fought the women. After that I started fighting for me and my sanity instead. Things still got to a point where I was starting to believe that Martrell had given the bitches my phone number. That's what had to be going down. I wasn't the most friendliest person. It seemed like every few days another female was calling me to put me up on game about Martrell. I finally got tired of it and told his ass we were done. I know he figured this would be like the other times I took him back but, I was done for real. He was still talking about something that I wasn't listening too. I needed to get off the phone with him because the longer we stayed on the phone the more his hope of us getting back together grew.

"Martrell," I called his name to stop him from talking.

"What's up baby girl?" He asked.

"I'm not your baby girl nigga so don't even try it. We're not getting back together but there's one thing I want you to do for me," I said with a big smile on my face.

"You know I'll do anything for you," he said sounding all hopeful and shit.

"I need you to kiss my ass and stop fucking calling me," I said ending the call.

I laughed as I fell back on my bed. I know he was over there pissed but, he got us here not me. Getting up to find me something to wear. Retail therapy was definitely needed along with getting my phone number changed again.

CHAPTER 2

Chaos

"Who sent you?" The old nigga I had tied to the chair asked.

"As long as I get paid on time I couldn't care less who sent me. You don't need to think about their name. It ain't like you're gonna get out of here to get your revenge," I chuckled.

These people killed me even though it was my job to kill them. I never asked for names or reasons, none of that mattered to me. I only cared about my money. As long as I got my deposits for my services I didn't give a fuck about anything else.

"How much did they pay you? I'll pay you triple whatever it is. I have a bunch of money, cars, vacation spots in the Caribbean. You name it and you'll have it just don't kill me," he pleaded.

I took my gun from the side holster I had it in. Not once did I think that getting inside of this guys house would be this easy. If he wasn't sitting here trying to bargain for his life I would've thought he was waiting for me by the way he was just sitting at the table when I came in. Most of the time when I did a job I had to break in or sneak up on the target. This one right here had the damn door open. It wasn't unlocked, the door was wide the fuck open. I was dressed in one of those plastic suits with my hands and shoes covered as well as my head. I was always careful that's why everyone who wanted someone done in came to me first. I know I'm not the only hit man in town but, I know that I'm the first choice.

He's the only one in the house and he was sitting at the table face down in a pile of cocaine. I had to slap his ass for him to even lift his head up. Once I got him tied up in the chair that he was sitting in, I closed and locked the front door. Since he was zoned out I did what I could do which is sit my ass on his couch and look at his TV. Now he was just coming out of whatever the hell he had going on. I know I could've killed him and just headed out but, where's the entertainment in that. I didn't have shit to do tonight so why not fuck with the man a little bit before I kill 'em.

"Fuck the Caribbean, I hate the fucking beach. All that sand and shit gets in every fucking thing. It takes days for me to get rid of all that shit," I told him.

I could tell by the look in his eyes that he was trying to think of something else that would persuade me to walk away from this job.

"I can't believe he sent a fucking kid after me," the mark said.

I ignored that comment because I know I looked young because I was young. I wasn't a fucking kid though. I'm twenty-six years old so he could miss me with that kid shit. I've been hearing that all my damn life. I didn't like being called a kid when I was one. That shit really pisses me off now.

"Guess you're gonna get killed by a kid then. How does that feel to ya?" I asked him.

"Tell him he's gonna rot in hell for this. He should've done it himself, fucking Punta," he went on and on.

"I thought you didn't know who sent me. Now you're calling

names and shit. Pick a side man either you know or you don't. It still doesn't matter because you're dying either way" I told him.

Realizing that me and this man could sit here and go back and forth all night I got up and untied him. With my gun to his head he was still scared to move.

"What are you doing?" He said with a shaky voice.

"Don't be acting stupid we both know why I'm here," I told him.

"I thought you were going to kill me. What are you doing now? Why all the talking? Just kill me and get it over with. That's what you're here for right, then do it. Shoot me now," he said still sounding scared.

"Sit your ass down and sniff up the rest of that coke," I said standing next to the table.

"I don't do it all the time. Just sometimes for the stress," he pleaded.

"Who do you think you're fooling? You have a pile of coke on your table in your house but, you only do the shit from time to time. Put ya nose down there and sniff," I told him as I cocked the gun pointing it at him.

I watched as he sniffed and cried. This had to be the weirdest job I had to do so far. I've been doing this killing shit since I was fourteen. I've done all types of shit just to make money. He called himself sniffing slowly as if that was going to change anything. That was one thing that I always found intriguing. When a person is out in the public they act like they're one of the baddest, toughest people in the world. Then when they're one on one with someone they know is a killer they'll be ready to pimp out their parents, grandchildren, kids, dog, cat, and even sign over the deed to their house just to stay alive. It was wild to me that death is the only guarantee in life but, when faced with death folks get scared shitless. Yes, there were a few that were thorough and didn't break but, I could count them on my hands.

"I don't wanna snort anymore. I don't feel right," he said with slurred words.

"You're not finished. Sniff it all up," I told him.

Watching him I knew that he was way past fucked up. He started mumbling to himself and shit. Then he sat straight up, his eyes were glassy as hell, his nose was bleeding, and suddenly his face went down on the table with so much force that it shifted the pile of coke that was on the table. I stood over him I pushed his head a little bit with the gun barrel. He didn't move. I checked for a pulse with my gloved right hand. There was nothing. I looked around the dining room and living room of the house to make sure I didn't leave anything behind. I took one last look at the dead man with his face planted in the pile of cocaine. I walked out I was sure to leave the door wide open being that it was that way when I got there.

Whenever I completed a job I had to go to the strip club or any club just to wind down. It was perfect that I was covered in plastic, that helped keep my clothes underneath spotless. I drove to the other side of town pulled up to an elementary school after pulling off the plastic that was covering my clothes and put them in the trash. I also threw a match in to burn it all up. Pulling off once the fire was going good I headed right for the strip club. A little bit of head and liquor will relax me just fine. I was only about twenty minutes away from the seven cities low-budget version of Magic City. There were some good looking strippers there but, none of them were Cardi B or Joseline. My mission tonight was a good nut and a good buzz. I parked my car in the parking lot of the car lot next door. Magic City was known to be the site for fights, shootings, even a few bitter ass girlfriends had come up there to fuck up their nigga's cars. I didn't need my car getting any damage done to it behind something I had no dealings with. It was a known fact that some people can't hold their alcohol that was the one thing I was hoping didn't happen. However, a quiet night at the strip club was a bogus ass wish but, I was wishing it.

"Hey Chaos what a nice surprise," one of the strippers said as I walked in.

"What's up," I replied not looking to see which stripper it was.

There were more hey's and how you doing's as I made my way through the club.

"Oh shit ladies we got my nigga Chaos in the house. Y'all strippers better get those pussy's fresh. We all know when Chaos drops through he drops that cash on y'all's ass," the ignorant ass DJ said.

I had to laugh at him because he always was saying something off the damn wall. I took my seat at an empty table. The place wasn't crowded but, there was a nice sized crowd in here.

"What can I get you Chaos?" One of the waitresses name Lisha asked.

"Hey Lisha get me a bottle of Remy," I told her.

"Coming right up," she said with a smile and went to go get my shit.

"What up Chaos?" My homie Dru said as he sat down.

"What up? I didn't see you when I came in. How long you been here?" I asked.

Dru was a chill ass dude. He wasn't in the street but, he had the respect for the streets. He used to be an amateur boxer but, that shit came to an end when his parents got killed. They were caught up being in the wrong place at the wrong time and got hit by a car that the cops were chasing. That was the saddest shit ever. The rest of the family chipped in and got a lawyer. They sued the city and received an undisclosed amount of money. Being that his dad was his trainer and coach he never stepped in the ring again. He was still knocking niggas out though. We were always cool it was just the niggas he usually ran with I didn't vibe with them at all. It wasn't anything that I would call beef, the niggas just didn't fuck with me, so I didn't fuck with them either.

"Tony and Rocco are here with me. Tony's fucking some bitch in the bathroom. His cheap ass didn't want to pay for a private room so that's where they went. Rocco's at the table by himself, over there,"He pointed to where Rocco was but, I didn't look up because Rocco was the main one I didn't fuck with. That nigga always looked at me funny and shit. I was just waiting for him to get his balls off the ground and come tell me what the fuck his problem was with me. As far as I knew I hadn't fucked the nigga's girl or sister. He and I didn't run with the same people. I hadn't done shit to him so fuck him.

"I keep telling you those niggas was gonna have you in some shit one day. Doing the shit that he's doing out here is only going to fall on the people around him. He's gonna expect you to take the fall for him when and if the time comes. The question you need to ask yourself is do you believe him or any of the other niggas you hang around won't have you take the fall for whatever shit they get in, if that helps them get off. If you can't say that they'll ride for you through the mud then there isn't no need for you keep them niggas around," I told Dru.

There were times everybody would tell Dru that Rocco's ass was bad news and Tony wasn't any better. However, Dru was one of those people that were loyal to a fault. I just hope misguided loyalty didn't send him to the cemetery with his parents. He had my respect for not flipping on his man but, if everybody is warning you loyalty or not his ass would be cut the fuck off.

"What happened between y'all?" Dru asked.

"Ain't shit happen your mans is just a bitch. I don't say two words to the nigga but, he always looking at me like I knocked up his baby mama. You gotta ask him what's his beef. That's your mans he'll tell you. When he do hit me up I'd like to know too. I don't mean to be rude and shit but, take your ass back over there. I gotta bust a nut before I head home," I told him.

"No doubt. I'm not gonna fuck up your groove. I'll see ya around Chaos," Dru said when he left the table.

"Here's your bottle Chaos," Lisha said putting the bottle on the table with a glass and a bucket of ice.

"Thanks baby, what time you take your next break?" I asked.

She giggled just like she always did. Lisha was quiet but her head game was fucking epic. I liked dealing with her because she didn't hang with a bunch of birds or run her mouth for clout. She was so good at keeping shit on the low I even tossed some money her way just because.

"I can get away after I take this tray back to the kitchen," she said licking her lips.

"Meet me at my car it's parked in the lot next door," I told her.

"Okay big daddy," she said with a smile.

I watched her walk away. Some times I wondered if her pussy was as good as her mouth. It wasn't like I would ever find out because fucking her would be crossing a line for me. If I put this dick on her she would damn sure change the way she was moving. I for damn sure didn't need that. I took the bottle off the table and headed for the door.

"Yo, Bear, go chill at my table I gotta take a call right quick," I said to one of the bouncers as I handed him my bottle. I wasn't gonna leave my bottle on the table for niggas to steal or for them to drop some shit in my bottle. Yeah, I was low-key paranoid. He gave me a nod with a smirk and went to the table.

I got to the car and waited for Lisha to bring her ass. She was taking a long ass time. There was a tap on my window. It was Lisha with a big ass smile on her face. There's nothing better than a female that shows she's excited to suck ya dick. That shit is priceless.

CHAPTER 3

Paradise

Last night I ended up right where I was supposed to end up and that's in my bed. I was going to go shopping to relax my mind but, my choice of watching a movie before leaving turned into me falling asleep on the couch. I needed to get myself together to go see about Auntie Gail. I haven't been to see her in a long time. I could only stomach her in small doses. She had some weird jealous thing between her and my mother. Ivy and I had asked mom what happened to make them act like they do with each other. The only thing my mom would say was that not everyone will be happy about your happiness. I didn't understand what she meant by that until I got older. Auntie Gail was never one to say good job or congratulations for anything or to anybody. It didn't matter how big or small she always had some snide remark. I remember when I told her that I wasn't going to go to college but, I was gonna start doing make-up full time. After looking at me like I had lost my mind she told me that make-up was a hobby. Then she threw in that she hopes I do halfway good at it because she knew I didn't want to move back home with my parents. Yup, that's what she said no words of encouragement or nothing.

She was my mother's only sister and the mother of the only three first cousins that I had and she couldn't even congratulate me. When Ivy finally told everyone about her and Toxin being a couple, she was even worse. Good old Auntie Gail was nice enough to tell my sister that Toxin never wife's a female. Even if he did wife her that she would have to deal with side chic's and outside babies for as long as they would be together. Poor Ivy had to leave or she was going to mollywop our auntie. Her negative outlook kept me away for this long. I had nothing pressing to do so heading over there for at least ten minutes was the plan. When I pulled up I saw my cousin Rocco's challenger in the front. I rolled my eyes because he was just like his mother. If he spent more time working on getting his own shit he wouldn't have time to hate on everyone else. Rocco hated on any one that had a better car, better status, better hoes, and better whatever compared to his. I've told him over and over to go out here and get his own. The nickel and diming that he was doing wasn't going to get him anywhere ever in life. Instead of listening to the people around telling him that he's doing shit ass backwards he would continue to do what he was doing but, talk about everyone else around him that was doing better. Even with all the hating they had going on they were still family. That's why I went to check on Auntie Gail from time to time. Ivy didn't fuck with them at all. I pulled up cut the car off and went to knock on the door praying for the lord to shut my mouth the entire time.

"Oh if it ain't my niece, I haven't seen you in a long time," Auntie Gail said looking past me at my car that was parked next to the curb. "Is that a new car?" She asked knowing damn well it ain't new.

"Nah, that's the same car," I answered as I walked past her into the house.

"Mmhm, I guess it being clean makes it look different. That's a nice car though how much does it run you a month," she asked.

"Where is everybody? It's quiet around here," I say changing the subject.

"You're just like your mama. Always scared that somebody's gonna ask for some money. I ain't never asked you for no money and I ain't now. Keep that monthly payment to yourself then. Just make sure when you can't make the payment don't call me to help," she said making me roll my eyes.

"I'll be sure to scratch you off the list then. Where's Rocco?" I asked.

"He's in his room. If you go up there knock first ain't no telling what he's doing up there," she said with a smirk.

"Nah, I'll pass on that. I just came by to see how y'all been doing. I'm gonna head out though and let you get back to what you were doing," I said walking back out of the door.

"Tell your mama that I'm still alive with high blood pressure. It's a shame my own sister doesn't come see me. I know it's y'alls daddy's fault. He got her over there thinking she's better than us little people. I never thought dick could change my sister but, you live and you learn. Is your sister still with Toxin or did he use and lose her ass already," she said.

"Nobody comes over here but, me because they don't understand that you have to be suffering from some undiagnosed mental condition. The shit that comes out of your mouth is un-fucking-necessary. My mom doesn't come over because she doesn't want any of the hateful demon that's all in here on her. It doesn't have anything to do with her thinking she's better than anyone. My mama knows she doesn't have to keep dealing with your bullshit. If you would focus on yaself and not everyone else you would know that your wig is on backwards, that mustache you're rocking needs tending too, and that no one in their right mind still has plastic runners on the floor to match the plastic on the furniture. You need help Auntie, like some serious medicated kind of help," I told her.

"Oh you call yourself telling me off little girl. Just like your damn mama. You all high and mighty now because you got that business of your own. One day you're gonna find yourself just like me," she said.

"It's sad that you still believe that dumb shit. If I ever stop doing makeup, I'll start another business. One thing I will never do is let myself get to the point of allowing myself to sit around a plastic ass house, with a backwards wig, Steve Harvey mustache, waiting on a state check so I can buy a pack of cigarettes. Auntie do you have a specific brand you get now or are you still doing the cheapest one the store has. I see why my mom and sister don't fuck with your hateful ass," I told her before walking out of the door.

I got in my car and had to take a few deep breaths. I wasn't coming to see her ass no damn more. I was praying for the wrong thing. I should've been praying for her to lose her voice instead. Instead of heading straight to see Ivy and Toxin I stopped by the corner store to get my first Pepsi of the day. I had a mild Pepsi addiction but, they had to be ice cold in order for me to drink it. Ivy always says that it's a weird addiction to have but, I'm normal compared to the people on TV eating toilet paper and shit. When I walked in the store there was weird ass Chaos talking to some female but looking at me just like always. I don't know what his problem was but, one day I'm gonna ask his sexy ass. Even though he was always weird around me I couldn't deny one bit how damn sexy he is. He was tall I would say around six feet one inch. His skin didn't appear to have any blemishes on it which is strange for a guy. He was a light chocolate brown, nice full lips, and the most beautiful eyelashes I had ever seen. His eyes were a real light brown, his hair was in a regular tapered low cut. He had one big ass diamond in his right ear. So yes the nigga was fine as fuck. I had to give his ass the 'when a nigga looking' walk. Since all he wanted to do was stare at me I was gonna give his ass a show.

"You just gonna look at her ass like I'm not standing here?" The chic asked him.

"If you feel some type of way move the fuck around then. Either you gonna finish talking or not, it doesn't matter to me.

How you gonna get mad because I'm looking at her ass? Did you see how plump that mother fucker is? You had to notice because your ass is on paper thin for sure," I could hear him respond before the store's door closed.

I couldn't help laughing at what I heard. That nigga would never talk to my ass like that. Everybody knew that Chaos was a dangerous nigga but, he still wouldn't carry me like that with his disrespectful ass. I got my Pepsi, paid for my shit and when I came out he was still talking to the dumb ass girl that he was talking to before.

"Here her ass go," she said making me smile.

"Shut the fuck up we just had this discussion. When I see a ass I like I'm gonna look. Period, point blank, if you don't like the shit we can go back to being full fledged strangers," he told her.

"Full fledged strangers? We stopped being strangers when I put your dick in my mouth," the girl said proudly.

"Nah, we was still strangers you just suck dick good enough to do it again. I still don't know shit about you and you don't know shit about me. I know your name and what that mouth do. Anything beyond that I have no fucking clue. I have your number saved in my phone as 'the backup blow broad'. I just put my dick in ya mouth from time to time nothing more and nothing less," he told her.

See that shit right there, her ass was cool with the way he was talking to her. I don't care if they had an understanding or not. He would never do no shit like that to me. He's fine and all but, ain't no way in hell. Yeah, he could keep right on dealing with silly bitches like that. I kept laughing as I got in the car and yeah his ass was damn sure looking.

CHAPTER 4

Chaos

"I can't believe how you just embarrassed me like that. Damn I thought we were better than that," the chic said.

I was too busy looking at the tail lights on Paradise's car to even reply to her ass. I just shook my head and went in the store. I was only coming in here to get some skittles and a soda. I didn't see whatever the fuck her name was as soon as I got out of the car. That's the problem with these chics you let them suck ya dick a few times and they think they're your best fucking friend. After I paid for my shit her ass was still standing next to my damn car.

"What you still out here for?" I asked her.

"I want to make sure we're still good," she said.

"Still good? Who told you we were good in the first damn place? You got a mouth and I gotta dick that likes to be sucked. Does that sound like we're best friends to you? That's what's wrong with y'all females these days. Tell you what, your ass is off the team. When you see me out and about just forget what my dick feels like in ya mouth," I told her as I got into my car. Of course, her ass didn't move. "You got three seconds to either move or get ran the fuck over," I told her after rolling my window down. Her non-counting ass didn't move so me being a man of my word I put my car in reverse and backed the fuck out. She stumbled away from the car looking like she was surprised that I had pulled out with her still leaning on my shit.

"Chaos, really!" She screamed.

I didn't say shit to her, I just gave her a head nod and went on about my way. Dealing with all these chics are draining the hell out of me. It was insane that they would even think because they suck my dick that we were in some kind of relationship. These broads were doing the absolute most out here for no damn reason. She know damn well I ain't lay no claim to her so why would she even try to lay claim to me even if she said we were only friends.

After leaving the store I went to grab me something to eat before I took my ass home. I needed some rest but, it wasn't like I had been doing anything. I needed to let all the chic's on the team marinate on seeing me for a while. I ended up at this little burger spot that made the best burgers in town in my opinion. I walked up to the register and before I even opened my mouth the chic at the register was looking at me like I had asked her ass to marry me or something.

"Heyyy, Chaos, what can I get for you today?" She asked looking star struck.

I was used to chics acting like I was a star but, it was seriously getting old.

"Yeah ahh, give me a number one with cheese and a large iced tea," I told her for some reason she started giggling.

"That'll be seven dollars and sixty-two cents," she said still fucking giggling.

I handed her the money. Just like all the other chic's around here she took to damn long to take the money. Although I was irritated I just chuckled the shit off.

"Bitches stay on that nigga dick. He ain't nothing special though, he bleed just like everyone else. It ain't like he's a fucking star or some shit. It's fucking pathetic," a familiar voice said from behind me. I turned around to look the nigga in the face.

"You got something you wanna say Rocco. I'm just asking because it seems like you got a lot to say when I'm not around or when my back is turned. Now, I'm here looking you in the face like the MAN that I am speak your peace," I told him.

The entire restaurant was on hush mode. You could hear a pin drop in that bitch while we all waited to see what this bitch ass nigga had to say.

"Nigga, I'll speak my damn peace anywhere I fucking please. You don't run shit over here. You might think everybody around here is scared of you but, fuck you. I ain't scared of shit especially your punk ass, bitch,"he said with a smile like he was really doing something.

I looked at the two clowns that he had with him. They looked like they wanted him to shut the fuck up.

"What did I do to you? Did I fuck ya girl or let her suck me off? I'm saying I had to do some disrespectful shit for you to hate a nigga that you don't fucking know," I said.

I was sure to walk up on him eliminating whatever space was between us. I didn't want to fuck up these folks restaurant but, it was looking like that's what was about to go down. I wasn't backing down from this nigga. He had already put his foot in his damn mouth. His next move was gonna make or break his rep. Niggas like Rocco cared about what other people thought.

"This nigga ain't shit. Come on y'all let him make it today," one of his dudes said.

"Nah, you've been quiet all this time keep it that way. Say what you gotta say Rocco because the next time I see you it can be whatever," I told him.

"Bitch made niggas," was all he could get out.

I hit him with a left hook followed by a jab from my right. There was a chance that his boys would jump in but, I wasn't gonna stop until I couldn't swing anymore. He tried to swing at me but, I could see my hits had that nigga feeling drunk. I hit him with a gut shot after ducking another weak ass attempt to hit me. He tackled me down to the ground confirming he was indeed the bitch that he accused me of being. I still held my fucking own though. Rolling around on the ground with him taking and giving shots back to back. I finally got enough room to head butt the nigga so that's what I did. The impact of the head butt dazed him a little bit. While he was dazed I punched his ass twice and he was out like a light. I stood to my feet. The first thing I did was look to see why his boys didn't jump my ass. I was fully expecting that shit. I smirked when I saw that some of the niggas that were eating in the restaurant had formed a circle around us. I didn't know these niggas well, I don't think I did. One of them looked at me when I looked at him.

"Sup, we couldn't let them jump you after all the shit that their homie was talking. Somebody gotta live by a code these days," he said.

"Good looking out. I appreciate that shit. All I wanted to do was get some fucking food. What's your name man?" I asked.

"I'm Prince, that's my brother Phantom, and our cousin Pharaoh," he said they all gave me a head nod.

"Y'all from around here?" I asked. I couldn't remember if I saw them around or not. "Put ya number in my phone or call my shit either way it doesn't matter to me. Hit me up if you need some help. I know you know who I am," I said.

"Everybody around here knows you Chaos. That's the main reason we couldn't let you go out like that. He shouldn't have said all that bullshit anyway. I can't stand a hating ass nigga," he said as he did what I asked and gave me my phone back.

"Chaos your food is ready," the chic at the register said. She wasn't giggling and all that other shit now though. I guess the fight took her flirty mood away.

"Thanks, is the owner here?" I asked.

"No, she doesn't come in on weekends unless she has too. Is there something I can help you with?" She said smiling. And just like that the flirty shit was back.

"Nah, I'm cool on all the extra shit. Thanks for the food

though. Sorry about the shit that went down though," I told her as I took my food and walked out of the door.

Walking to my car I could see Rocco and his boys standing a few feet away. From the look on Rocco's face I knew that fight only made the situation worse between us. Too bad he was a bout to keep getting his ass kicked behind his bullshit ass feelings. Too bad for him I had nothing but, time on my hands. We could do this shit everyday if he wanted to.

After fighting Rocco I didn't feel like goin home so I decided to stop by the barber shop. It was always packed with niggas that just didn't want to go home. I figured I'd go in there for a while and shoot the shit with them before going home. I was tired before I ran into Rocco's ass. I still couldn't understand what his damn problem was with me. All that shit he was spitting just sounded like he was fucking jealous. Niggas outside looking in always feel some type of way about the shit other people have. I went through hell to get where I am now but, he wasn't looking at it like that. Oh well, there ain't shit I can do about that except be ready for his ass. Usually when you beat a niggas ass they come back with their friends to jump you or they come at you with a gun to kill you. I was ready for either but, I doubt if Rocco was and he's the one starting all this shit.

"Nigga, what the hell you doing walking in here like you just left the carwash but, my phone blowing up talking about you're fighting at the burger spot," The owner and my barber Ace said laughing.

"All I wanted to do was get me something to eat. Everything that happened wasn't on me. That nigga's always had a problem with me. I haven't done shit to that man he's just a bitch," I said as I sat in one of the empty barber chairs.

"Tell me why you was just playing with that boy. I saw the shit just like everyone else. The difference is that I KNOW you. You weren't serious about that damn fight. You still beat his ass but, not like Chaos should've. What the fuck was that all about?" Ace asked.

"I wasn't doing shit so why not entertain the clown. He ain't shit for real but, now he knows it for sure," I told him.

I used the hand sanitizer that was on the station before I opened my food up. They all were laughing and talking about how the fight was all over social media. It only happened like fifteen minutes ago and it was already getting shared and re-shared by everyone. As usual they all exchanged what might've been said before the recording started. I just let them talk I never chimed with what was said because it was all some high school type of shit to me. The shit went left when he got disrespectful.

"You not gonna settle this dumb ass debate and just say what the man said to make you hit his ass?" Ace asked me.

"Y'all niggas are funny as fuck. Y'all really wanna know?" I asked.

"These niggas got a bet going on what he actually said. The only way the winner is gonna win you gotta tell us what he said," Ace said.

I shook my head because these niggas would bet on any damn thing. One time they sat around betting on which little boy that came in the shop could read or not. The shit was funny as hell to watch.

"He called me a bitch ass nigga," I said.

"Yeah nigga, pay me my damn money. I told you niggas what he said," One of the guys said loud as hell from his seat. I fell out laughing because he was hype as hell right now. I knew that coming here would lighten up my mood. These niggas were always with the shits and giggles. I stayed with them laughing, joking, shooting dice, and not thinking about the dumb shit I had to deal with today until closing time . That's when I took my ass home and crashed out after I took a shower.

CHAPTER 5

Paradise

"Yo, what the hell is going on around here. Yo, wake your big head ass up. You need to go home because this ain't it lil sis," Toxin screamed as he hit my foot until I opened my eyes.

"It's a damn shame I can't get my beauty sleep because of niggas with attitudes at the moment," I sat as I sat up to stretch.

I didn't mean to fall asleep at their house but, I got caught up looking at movies with the kids. They didn't even bother to wake me up. I was gonna get them, they should've at least told me to go in one of the guest rooms.

"You damn right I got an attitude. I can't walk around naked because you couldn't take your ass home. I forgot all about Ivy telling me your big head ass was on the couch. Why you over here? Your cable out? Lights off?" Toxin's dumb ass asked laughing.

"Don't play you know I pay all my bills," I told him rolling my eyes.

"You don't look hung over so what gives? Why are you on my couch instead of in your bed?" He asked.

"I saw your little weird ass friend yesterday at the corner store," I told him. He balled his face up but, I could tell he was wondering who I was talking about. "Chaos, I saw Chaos last night. He was talking to some bird and they got into it because he was worried more about my ass than whatever she was talking about. When I came out he did the same shit again. I ain't know he was so fucking rude. I thought all your friends had manners," I told him.

"You must've said something to him or something. I asked you why you ain't go home not who you saw at the damn corner store. As for Chaos that nigga is complex as fuck. He is who he is because life made him that way. If he ain't say nothing directly to you then why you worried about him being rude to the next chic?" He asked me.

"I'm not worried about him at all. It was just bothersome to hear how he was talking to her," I told him. He just stared at me like he was trying to figure a puzzle or something out. I started to feel uncomfortable with how hard he was staring at me. "Why are you looking at me like that?" I asked.He just kept looking then he smirked.

"Nothing, are you going home or do I have to cook for your big head ass too?" He asked changing the subject.

"No, don't do that changing the subject shit tell me why you were looking at me like that," I demanded.

"I don't know what the fuck is up with you and Chaos but, y'all will get it together soon enough," he said getting up and walking to the kitchen. I got up and was stomping right behind him.

"Chaos and I? There is no Chaos and I. He's weird as hell. All he does is stare at me. He never talked to me. He just stares like a creep," I told him.

"You got him shook lil sis," Toxin said laughing.

"How can I have a man shook that I never even said two words to?" I asked.

"That night at the club when I came to y'all table. He was looking at you then. You threw him off with you tried to make the straw in your drink cum. The way you was sucking on the straw had him so stuck that he just left," Toxin told me.

I tried to remember that part but, the way Ivy and I were drinking there's no telling what all I did. I shook my head because I had not one word that I could say to explain me doing that to a straw. It was kind of funny when I thought about it so I laughed.

"Chaos kills people well, I heard he kills people so why do he act all shook around me. I don't believe you I think he's just a fucking creep and you're trying to take up for him by making me look crazy. I'm not crazy," I told him.

"Both of y'all have some unresolved issues but, that ain't none of my business. If he hasn't pushed up on you then, why you so bothered by him?" He asked me.

I didn't have an answer for that and that fact alone pissed me off. Any other guy I wouldn't pay him any mind and keep on keeping on. Why did I feel the need to address Chaos' behavior? Why was it when I saw him I got this funny feeling throughout my body? This was insane how is this man affecting me but, at the same time we don't speak a word to one another. The shit was crazy.

"I don't have an answer for you Toxin. The shit is crazy as hell," I told him.

"Don't sit over there and use all those brain cells trying to figure it out. Everything happens when it's supposed to happen. You haven't figured it out because it ain't time for you to figure it out yet. Trust me when the time comes you'll have a full understanding of what the hell is going on with you two," Toxin told me.

"Let me find out you know about some stuff," I said smiling.

"I know a lot don't let the tattoos and the rep fool you. I'm a lot of things but dumb and not observant ain't one of them . There's no way I could have all my shit together to snag your sister and be a dumb nigga all at the same time. We all know Ivy ain't even going out like that. On the real though stop trying to figure out what you're not supposed to understand yet. When the time comes you'll know," he told me.

I wanted to say something smart or crazy to him so bad but, I couldn't find anything to say. Toxin was a good look for my sister. Maybe he was right and I should just chill and let shit happen how it's supposed to.

"Can I take a shower before I leave here?" I asked.

"You got clothes here?" He asked.

"No, I have a bag of clothes and stuff in my trunk," I said. He looked at me and started laughing.

"You got a damn hoe bag man. I ain't know you was doing it like that. You ain't got nothing do you?" He said still laughing.

"I have a size eight and a half that's ready to go up your ass. Don't try to play me like that. That bag is in the car because sometimes I'm too tired to go home after working a long job. Everything ain't about being a hoe or getting some dick," I told him.

"Tell my black ass anything. Your thot ass, yeah man go get ya thot bag. I hope you take a real damn shower too. Don't wash ya ass in my fucking sink man. You can be a thot all you want to but, be the best thot and the cleanest thot out here. If you a nasty thot it'll reflect on me even worse because you're family," Toxin told me.

"Fuck you Toxin. You get on my damn nerves man," I told him laughing.

"What the hell is going on down here? What are you two going off on each other about?" Ivy said coming down the steps.

"She thinks I can't see she wanna put it on Chaos. He wanna do her just like she wanna do him but, they're too busy asking my black ass about each other," Toxin said.

"He's lying sis. Ain't nothing popping off with me and no damn Chaos. That nigga just likes to look at the merchandise not touch it," I said sticking my tongue out at the end and doing a little dance.

"So you are for sale? Damn I got the good sister," Toxin said kissing Ivy. She was laughing with him. The whole scene was getting on my nerves. I know Toxin was playing but, it still stung a little bit.

"Stop trying to play my sister. She's not for sale, don't make me hurt you in here. My sister is a beautiful, independent black woman, if she wants to hop on a dick every once in a while that's her business. She ain't in it for the money though, don't do her like that," Ivy said speaking up for me.

I smiled because I knew she wasn't going to keep letting him play me to the left like that. Ivy was different about things like that when it came to me. She was always protecting me. Even with me going to see our Auntie she always tried to talk me out of it before I went because we all know how hateful she is. Here it is she's protecting me against the man I threw her under the bus for. They were great together though, even if the way they ended up together was a little out of the ordinary it didn't take away from them being meant to be together. They both looked to be so happy with each other. That was a happiness that I was slowly realizing that I would never get to have. I was okay with that but, seeing them together sometimes gave me false hope.

"It's all good I know he doesn't mean any harm he just likes giving me a hard time. I should've let y'all get together on y'all own but, y'all look so good together I don't have any regrets," I told her giving her a hug.

CHAPTER 6

Chaos

Sitting in the office of my carwash my eyes were starting to cross. It was getting late and I was still here checking the books. I may not have worked here everyday but, I damn sure liked to pop up on my shit and check the books. This carwash and the cleaners attached to it were the first businesses I purchased on my own. When I first brought this everyone thought I was doing it just to have something to do. However, this was the start of my legal empire. I wasn't gonna be a hit man all my life. I was planning on getting out of this shit by the time I turn thirty-five or forty would be the longest.

"Hey Boss, you're still here?" My manager Billy asked.

"Yeah, just going over the books and shit. It looks like you're getting the hang of this manager shit," I told him.

Billy wasn't always the manager. During the first eight months of opening I went through four managers. Billy was a worker from the beginning. During the time in-between me firing one and hiring another I would let him run shit. After firing the last one I just gave the position to him. He's been rocking the hell out of it ever since. I still did pop ups but, now when I did them I didn't end up beating somebody's ass. The other managers had a problem with stealing. It didn't matter what they stole if they could take it they would. I even had one steal six five gallon buckets of washing detergent. The stupid part came when he took it to Ace's barbershop to try to sell em. It wasn't until then I found out that his ass had a damn habit that he was hiding from everyone including his wife and kids. Then there was another one that was a chic named Nunie her ass was too busy fucking the customers to get any work done. I came in here one day to find her bent over getting tore out the frame. I shot the dude fucking her in the ass and her in the shoulder. I didn't want to kill her but, she needed to learn some damn manners. The only people that can fuck at work are the fucking owners.

"After seeing so many come and go I was determined to get this shit right. Aye can I ask you something?" Billy asked.

"You just did but, what's up?" I asked looking at him.

"Is it true you and Rocco are beefing? I heard about the fight yesterday," he said.

I leaned back in the chair looking at him. If he was asking me about that bullshit that means everybody was talking about it now. I hated when shit like this happened. Most of the time situations ended up way worse than what it should've been. All because of niggas and bitches running their mouths and getting all the information wrong.

"We fought but, I don't have no beef with his simple ass. The nigga just don't like me," I shrugged.

"If you don't have a beef with him then why y'all fight?" He asked.

"We fought because although I don't care about the nigga one way or the other. He got his ass beat because he's disrespectful as fuck. You can't go around being disrespectful if you can't hold your own. He was hoping that his boys would jump in but, some niggas saw how lopsided the situation could get and stepped in. What did you hear?" I asked just out of curiosity .

"Just that you and him got into it. Rocco's claiming that you started the shit with him. I knew that wasn't the case because you finish shit you don't start it. Not as long as I've known you, anyway. Something just didn't seem right. You be sure to keep an eye out for Rocco. We all know he's not the one to take an ass kicking lightly no matter how much he deserved the shit," Billy told me.

I had to nod my head because he was right. Rocco was a fucking punk with a big ass mouth. He was the poster child for letting your mouth get you into something that your ass can't handle. The thing I couldn't understand was how was he still walking around like he was the man when all he did was get his ass beat behind bullshit. The other thing I couldn't get was why the fuck was he coming at me all of a sudden. Granted the nigga has always been a hater from a distance but, now he had found some balls and heart from somewhere.

"You're right," I told him.

"I'm gonna go ahead and leave. Are you gonna be all right here by yourself?" Billy asked.

"Man get your ass out of here," I told him laughing.

Billy walked out shaking his head. Billy was a little older than me but he was cool as fuck. He came to work twenty minutes early and left on time. He did everything he had to do in between. If I didn't come check on the place from time to time he would still do what needed to be done. Did I trust him? No, I trusted the fact that he needed to keep his job though.

I left not too long after Billy did. I had to go by the mall before it closed to get the new Jordan's that came out this week. I had a good hour and a half to get to the mall and get to the store. I prayed that the broad Nikki was there working. I couldn't remember if she worked tonight or last night. I would find out when I get there. While I was driving to the mall my damn phone started ringing.

"Yeah," I answered.

"Will your ass stop looking at my damn sister-in-law? I thought I was gonna run into you at the barbershop but, your ass never showed up," Toxin said.

"Ain't nobody thinking about her," I told him.

"Well, stop not thinking about her, and looking at her ass at the same time then," he said laughing.

"Is this why you called me?" I asked pulling into the parking lot of the mall.

"Yeah, I don't know what your problem is or isn't with her but, it's fucking her head up. Leave her a lone," he said.

"How bad am I fucking her head up though?" I asked him.

When I didn't hear a response I looked at the phone and his ass had ended the call on me. I parked and walked in the mall. My mind kept going to what Toxin was saying about me fucking Paradise's head up. Was she feeling a nigga? That's what it was; she had to be feeling me. I smiled at the thought of her mean ass digging me. When I walked into the store I looked around to see if I could see the chic that I fucked with from time to time that worked here named Nikki. Just my luck she was there but, she was working with this other broad that was sucking me off from time to time too. They both knew how I rolled but, I didn't know if they knew they were on the same team or not.

"Hello is there anything I can help you find today?" She asked.

"Yeah let me get a pair of the Jordan's that came out today size eleven. There should be a pair in the back for me. The name on them will be Chaos," I told her.

"Let me go back and see if they're back there," she said licking her lips at me.

Her freaky ass was probably trying to figure how she could suck me off without getting caught.

"How you been Chaos?" The other one said as she walked past me.

"I'm good. How you been?" I asked not really caring to hear the answer.

"If it ain't punk ass Chaos up in here, what up?" I heard Rocco ask from behind me,

I turned around to see he was alone this time.

"You fucking following me now? What you want a picture or something?" I asked.

"Nah, I just want to tell you that I'm gonna end your ass," he said trying to sound hard.

"Thanks for the special bulletin but, fuck you and that corny ass threat," I told him chuckling.

He pulled a gun out from the back of his pants, put it to my forehead. I could see he wasn't too sure about what he was doing just like before. He was trying to look hard and prove a point or some shit to motherfuckers who don't care about him or if he got his ass in trouble.

"Does this feel like a fucking bulletin to you?" He asked pressing the gun into my forehead harder.

The people in the store were running and hiding. I was looking this nigga in the eye. He had this gun to my head but, hasn't pulled the damn trigger yet. If he wanted to pull it so fucking bad what was the fucking hold up. I took two steps toward him with the gun still on my skin. He still didn't pull the trigger. He wasn't trying to kill me or anyone else today. I hit the gun out of his hand and followed up with a punch to his jaw. Here we were again fighting in public and shit. He was trying his best to get the upper hand on me but, that wasn't happening. After exchanging blows he got the bright idea to try to tackle me. He forced me against a display rack of clothes. I drove my elbow in to his spine which forced him to stop what he was doing. I hit him in the face with my knee making him fall to the ground. I then stood over him and started stomping him in the chest and head. My only mistake was that I hadn't paid attention to where the gun had gone. I had mine but, right now I didn't want to kill his ass, I just wanted him to stop this stupid shit that he had against me. He found some strength to hit me in my kneecap hard enough to make me stumble back.

"He's got the gun!" Someone yelled out.

I didn't look up to see if he had it or not but, what I did do was dive to the ground. Even though this isn't the route that I wanted to take I took my gun out and started shooting back in the direction that I knew Rocco was in. I was praying that I didn't hit any one but his ass. I managed to get out of the store and into the main hallways of the mall. This was the wildest shit I had ever been a part of we were having a damn shoot out in the fucking mall. I would duck behind kiosks ducking bullets and shit. I was trying to get a clear shot of him but, his punk ass was using innocent people to hide behind.

"They're shooting in the fucking mall!" I heard a voice that sounded like Paradise. I brushed it off thinking that my mind was playing tricks on me. "What the fuck you mean do I know whose shooting? Niggas with guns that's who's shooting!" She screamed. What the fuck was she doing in here? I was looking for Rocco's dumb ass but now here I am checking to see if Paradise is safe. I had stopped shooting but it took Rocco's dumb ass a few minutes to realize that he was shooting by himself. I was ducking behind everything so he wouldn't see me but, looking for Paradise at the same time. This shit was hard as fuck to do. I looked around and ended up finding her about three kiosk's down from where I was.

"Paradise!" I called her name to get her attention. She was balled up trying to hide herself from the shooters. Her head snapped around quick as hell.

"Oh hell nah, what the hell are you doing here?" She asked.

There haven't been any gun shots in about ten minutes so I could hopefully get her out of here safely. I grabbed her hand and took off running with her behind me.

CHAPTER 7

Paradise

"Slow the fuck down!" I yelled as I was being dragged by Chaos with his creepy ass. Where the fuck did he come from anyway.

"Nah, you just keep up we gotta get out of here," he told me.

It seemed like it took us forever to get out of the mall. Once we were out he took me to his car instead of to the police or some where else. I know he's not trying to use this situation to get him some ass from me. He definitely had me fucked up.

"Why the fuck didn't you take me to my car? I'm saying thank you for getting me out of there and shit but, We 're not fucking because of it. This ain't one of those movies where the chic falls in love with the guy who saves her and shit. This is real damn life. You and I are not fucking, Chaos," I told him. He needed to know he had me fucked all the way up.

He was speeding down the damn street like the police were after him when there wasn't a cop in sight. He looked pissed but, I was low-key scared to ask what the problem was.

"FUCK! MAN FUCK!" He yelled as he drove.

I don't know exactly what was going on but, whatever it was I wanted no parts of it.

"Let me out I'll figure out how to get home from here," I told him.

"I ain't putting you out on no fucking interstate shut the hell up and sit back. Just chill out I need to think and you're fucking up my concentration," he fussed.

"Nigga, I ain't one of those bitches that you can talk to any kind of way. Fucking with me will get you hit in the fucking jaw. I don't disrespect so I ain't getting disrespected. It doesn't matter to me if you're supposed to be some kind of killer or what the fuck ever it is that you do for money. The one thing no fucking body is gonna do is disrespect Paradise. Now check that shit," I told him.

I was so fucking pissed with him my fucking leg was shaking fast as hell. He didn't understand the caliber of woman he had in his damn car right now. That's all good though because I hope he was ready to learn because I was substitute teaching today. He was gonna have to get his shit together first of all with all that fucking rudeness that he had going on. The one thing that I didn't expect was the words that came out of his mouth when I finished going off on him.

"My bad I apologize," he said glancing over at me for a few seconds before turning back to the road.

Instead of saying what was on my mind I stayed quiet. We rode in absolute silence until we got to what I assumed was his house. It wasn't until we were getting out that I noticed that I didn't have my purse with me. No car keys, phone, identification, lip gloss, mace, or anything else I was out here bare assed.

"Shit," I said getting pissed off all over again.

"Man, what are you cussing about now?" Chaos asked me.

"I left my purse and everything I own was in it. I'm talking about my phone, money, ID, mace, lip gloss, shit everything. I'm gonna have a hard ass time getting everything replaced," I fussed.

It was gonna be more than hell putting my life back together.

How could I be so crazy to leave my purse like that? I was focused on what all I was going to have to do to get my stuff in tack and I look up to see Chaos just looking at me.

"Who were your credit cards with?" He asked.

"Umm Navy Federal, why do you need to know?" I asked.

He took out his phone and started texting. Not one time did he even try to explain why he asked or what he was doing. After he finished texting the phone rang.

"What up?" He answered. I rolled my eyes just out of natural reaction to hearing his voice. He listened for a few minutes then looked up at me. "Yeah, that's her, can you do it or not? I don't need all this extra shit right now. Did you text your sister and ask her?" He asked. When he felt me staring at him he walked away. I walked my ass right behind him. "Okay so the day after tomorrow," he said. He ended the call and tossed the phone on the counter top. When he stopped and turned around I was so close to him that we bumped into each other. "Damn, give me some room shit. We're gonna pick up your credit cards and ID tomorrow once I get the phone call. Now as for your female shit you're on your own for that. I'll pay for you to get a phone after we pick up your ID and shit," he told me.

"How the hell will I get a new ID without going to DMV? Who was that on the phone? How much will I have to pay you? I know ain't shit in life free especially when you're dealing with niggas like you," I told him.

When I said the 'niggas like you' part he stopped and smirked at me. I was ready for him to say some shit that would make me curse him out.

"You're welcome," he said then he turned back around and went on about his way. I was still behind him as he went in the kitchen to open the refrigerator. "Do you eat pork? Are you a vegetarian or one of them folks that eat only fish?" He asked looking over the opened refrigerator door.

"Huh?" Was all I could say. I was too busy looking at his eyes and lips. There needed to be a law against his lips being so fucking sexy. It was like just from looking at them I could tell they were soft. His eyes were so beautiful I could look at them motherfuckers all day and night. It was the smaller things about him that were the most attractive to me. Most women would be all about the gazillion tattoos he had, or how cut his body was. All of that added to his sex appeal but, it was just fluff to me.

"Yo, what the hell you got going on over there? I know you heard me talking to you but, you not giving me a damn answer. Fucking around with me your ass is gonna eat a mayonnaise sandwich," he said chuckling.

"There's that rude motherfucker," I said to him.

"Nah, I was being all social and shit with you but, you was over there zoned the fuck out. If you pay attention and respond when spoken to your stay here would be a lot better," he said still standing in the fridge. There ain't no way he has that much shit in there for him to be looking in there that long.

"Stay? Who said I was staying here with you? I'm taking my ass home," I told him.

"How the hell you gonna get there? You just realized you left your phone and purse back at the mall when all that shit happen. You can't call an Uber because you have no phone. You can't call for a ride because again you have no phone. Catching a bus is out of the question because they don't run all the way out here in the first place. If they did you don't have any money to get on there. Which also means you can't pay for a damn cab either? So where the hell you going just to end up looking like a runaway or some shit. If you get stopped by the cops their gonna take your ass downtown in the holding cell for however long it takes for them to finger print you. No ID, credit cards, phone, or anything else that's useful but, hey carry ya ass if you want," he told me.

"You think you have all the damn answers," I said rolling my eyes.

"I didn't say all that. I just make observations babygirl. I can only look at what you show me," he said licking his lips.

"I'm not a muslim or vegetarian,"I answered.

"Cool," was all he said.

I watched as he just kept doing what he was doing in the kitchen.

"I thought you were asking all that so you could fix me something to eat," I said.

"Nah, I'm a street nigga and a killer. The one thing I'm not is a fucking cook. It's some food in there go 'head and do the damn thing. A nigga like me did save ya life so you could cook my ass dinner to say thank you. There's some pork chops in there that I bought the other day. I was gonna get this old lady in the hood to cook them shits up for me. Since you're here you can do it," he said to me.

"Hold up you were in the fridge all that time but, you didn't get nothing out of it?" I asked.

"You do pay attention. I was just looking for something to drink. I asked if you were a particular eater because I needed to know if I was gonna have to go back to the store. Since I don't and you're not leaving until the day after tomorrow you can cook for a nigga. I miss a home cooked meal," he said rubbing his stomach.

"You really gonna expect me to cook? How do you know I can cook? I might fry the chicken and it tastes like cardboard," I told him.

"Yeah, okay I bet if you fry some chicken in here it won't taste like cardboard if you tried to make it that way. You a little too thick to not know how to cook," he told me.

"If that ain't a damn insult," I said shaking my head.

"Man, nah I ain't mean it as a insult it's just the truth. You not the type that can't cook. Anyway since you want to get all political and shit. Toxin told me you and your sister can cook y'all asses off so what's ya argument now?" He asked.

I rolled my eyes and made a mental note to lay Toxin's ass out. Why the hell would they be discussing me anyway?

CHAPTER 8

Chaos

The mood that best describes me right now is pissed the fuck off. I was this way for a ton of fucking reasons. I didn't get the fucking shoes I went to the mall for in the first place. It was fucked up that he was such a punk he tried that shit in a mall full of people. Anyone could've been hurt or worse. On top of that Paradise was one of those people. No matter how hard she tried to act I know she was scared and just as pissed as I was. Rocco needed to be counting his fucking days because I was about to do a fucking charity hit. By taking his ass out I would be giving back to the community. If I was here by myself I would go find his ass now but, now that Paradise was gonna be here for the next two days at least I couldn't leave her. If I did her ass would definitely leave before I came back. I probably should go check to see if she was climbing out of the window. She was seriously acting like she didn't want to be here. I just needed her to be safe. If she got hurt or worse and I was around Toxin would kill my ass for sure.

Toxin, Malcolm, Marsean, Jon-Jon, and even Satch when he was alive were all my big homies. They didn't know it but, I used to watch their movements like a hawk. They were the ones that laid the foundation for the man that Chaos was now. I owe them it all. It wasn't like I had male figure in my life period. So they were it for me. Even though the first body that I caught wasn't anything more than me being in the wrong place at the wrong time. A person could say that I was where I was supposed to be; it depends on your perception.

I was a young hard head around the age of fourteen. I was hanging out in the streets late as fuck. One of the guys I was hanging with that night had taken his step-dad's gun while he was at work. We snuck into this club well, not really because we snuck in every weekend. I think they were just letting us but, anyway one of the guys got into it with some old nigga. I was trying to get the niggas to leave because I had a feeling it would go downhill. They wanted to stay instead. When the club let out the old nigga wanted to finish what was started in the club. My homie passed me the gun thinking they were gonna box each other. The old guy pulled out a switch blade. I pulled the gun shot the nigga in the neck. Everybody ran around screaming and shit. I walked over to the guy laid out on the ground. I bent over looking at him in the eye as he took his last breath. I could hear the police sirens in the distance but, getting closer. I still didn't walk away until old dude stopped breathing. That was the night that Chaos was born.

Everyone started calling me Chaos because even with all the chaos going on around me I was still calm as fuck. I didn't run scream, yell or even shake during the entire incident. My homies were saying that I saved our friend's life. They were going on about how I should feel and all this other stuff but, I didn't feel shit. I took my first life and my life went on just like nothing had happen. I did however expect for the police to come to the house or to school to arrest me but that never happen. Even with the threat of the cops arresting me I wasn't scared or running. I did what I did and it was what it was.

"Do you have anything I can sleep in?" Paradise asked me.

I wasn't expecting to see her standing there in my robe. It

was big as hell on her but, still so fucking sexy. She had the collar of the robe below her shoulders. Her hair was soaking wet and hanging long, dripping and shit. Her skin was looking so pure that even though I was looking I couldn't find one blemish or bump. I just wanted to take the robe off her right now. I didn't care about finding her anything to wear she could wear me. I licked my lips as my dick grew.

"Nah, I ain't got nothing that's gonna fit you," I said as my eyes raped the fuck out of her right now. She rolled her eyes, kissed her teeth and stomped her foot. That only made her thigh creep out from under the robe. "You want a drink? I'm gonna make me a drink," I said getting up and walking away from her instead of doing what I wanted to do to her.

"A drink? You do realize I don't have anything on under this gigantic robe. What am I supposed to sleep in?" She asked.

"Man, just have a drink or two with me first. I finally came down off my adrenaline high," I told her.

"Oh yeah you're definitely on some bullshit. I'm not sitting around you drinking and naked. Stop playing with me nigga," she said.

"You need to just chill and relax," I said trying to calm her down. That only made her more amped. She was her sexiest when she was on ten. The way her eyes sparkled and she bit her bottom lip. Her ass was just the kind of feisty that I needed right now. She was the polar opposite of the females that I was used to dealing with. None of them would challenge me on shit that I said to them. If I tell them I didn't have shit for them to wear they would sleep naked with a big ass smile on their face. Not Pretty ass Paradise though, her ass would fight me if I said water was wet. She got a sneaky look on her face and turned to walk down the hallway. "Yo, where you going?" I asked her. Since she ignored me I went to see what she was doing. "I know you fucking lying," I yelled as I looked at this crazy ass girl go through the clothes in my closet.

"I know damn well I can find something here for me to sleep in. You've done lost all your little tiny ass mind thinking I'm gonna sleep in here naked. You got Paradise all the way fucked up," she said as she just randomly pulled shit down.

"Stop throwing my shit everywhere man. What the fuck is wrong with you?" I asked as I walked up on her.

She kept right on like she didn't hear or see me next to her. I grabbed her by her upper arm between her shoulder and her elbow turning her to face me. She was breathing all hard as the robe fell to the ground. I was supposed to be pissed with her about her fucking up my closet but we were gonna deal with that later. Right now I had some other shit to address.

"Let me go Chaos. If you can't give me a shirt then I can find one on my own," she said.

I took the shirt and wife beater that I had on off. I handed her the shirt.

"Here take this one," I told her.

The sexual tension in the air was on 5 trillion. It didn't help that I was caressing her bare nipple with my pinky of the hand that was holding the shirt out to her. Her breathing became erratic, her eyes closed as she licked her lips. I took the last step possible and covered her lips with mine. I let the shirt fall to the floor. My hands did the one thing they've been wanting to do since I had been seeing her around everywhere. Both of my hands were now entangled in her wet hair. It wasn't that I was checking to see if her hair was real or anything but, I just wanted my fingers in her hair. I would rather it was done while I was digging in her guts but, it'll happen soon enough. The only way this kiss would stop is because she was gonna stop it . I damn sure wasn't. She moaned and wrapped her arms around my bare back.

"Chaos, we can't do this," she said with the mouth that she was still kissing me with. I guess she just wanted to hear herself talk.

"Fuck yo nigga," I mumbled back in-between kisses.

Usually I would only be thinking about getting my dick sucked but, right now I was thinking about way more than that. My hand left from the top of her head down to her plump breasts. They felt like pillows or marshmallows. If I could stop kissing her I would be breastfeeding for damn sure. Everything about this crazy ass woman was driving me crazy. Her moaning to the feel of her skin beneath my fingers was turning me the fuck on. I had to have her. I pulled my pants down to free my dick from the unnecessary bondage of my pants and boxers. Now wasn't the time for forplay or love making. I was a beast hungry for this woman in front of me. I had to satisfy my hunger and worry about everything else later. With one hand I pushed everything off the shoe island in the middle of my closet. I turned Paradise around so her ass was right against my dick. I was kissing on the back of her neck and shoulders.

"Ahhh," she moaned as I caressed her pussy with two of my fingers on one hand. The other hand went to her throat. She was gonna learn one damn thing in this closet today.

"Don't get quiet now. Talk your shit Paradise," I said directly in her ear. She was going crazy but, not crazy enough to get the dick yet. I played with her pussy, slightly choked her, and licked her neck and ear at the same time. "Do you want this dick?" I asked her. I knew her stubborn ass was gonna try me by not saying anything but, I had time and nut today. She moaned again but, still no answer. I bit her earlobe and pinched her clit between my forefinger and thumb at the same time. Keep in mind I was still choking her too.

"Yessssss!" She yelled out finally.

"Good girl, open up for me," I whispered. She did as she was told and I eased my dick inside her.

"Ohhhhhh," she moaned.

"Damn, your pussy feel good. Feels like Paradise," I said.

I was trying not to squeeze her neck too hard but, the deeper I got in her pussy the tighter my hands got around her neck. She was wet as the fucking pacific. Poison is the only word I could use to describe her right now. I was trying not to go any faster than I was fucking her now but, that was not going to happen. She had to learn that I was the damn boss in here right now.

"Yes, Chaos, give me that dick," Paradise said trying to throw her pussy back on me.

"Stop that shit," I said smacking her on the ass. "The fuck you think this is. Just take this damn dick. It's good to you ain't it?" I asked smacking her ass again.

"Yes," she answered.

"Then stop doing too damn much and take it like I fucking tell you too," I said. I knew that last part was gonna have her talking shit back to me.

CHAPTER 9

Paradise

Yes, the dick is good but, it ain't that damn good. He still hasn't learned I'm not one of those other females. I'm not looking at his ass like he's the second coming. I'm all for talking good shit in the heat of the moment but, that shit he just said wasn't it at all.

"I know you heard me. Are you gonna be a good girl and do what daddy said?" He had the nerve to ask. See what I mean he's just doing too damn much right now.

"Mmmmm," I moaned. I was certainly pissed about how he was trying to carry me but, I had to get this nut right quick. I started rolling my hips in a circle as he barged in and out of my pussy. "How's that daddy?" I said all sexy like.

"Ahh hell man that's what the fuck I'm talking about. Do dat shit Poison Paradise? Damn, girl. Shit. Oh fuck!" He yelled out. His hand tightened on my waist.The pleasure of knowing that I had drove that nigga to the point of him not being able to hold his nut any longer made me reach my orgasm as well. "I can feel it babygirl. That's right let that shit go," he said as if he was tired as hell right now.

I waited a few minutes before I stepped away from him. He was standing in his same spot. He had one arm on the rod that the clothes were hanging on. I took in the beautiful disaster that was named Chaos. Just looking at him he was indeed a wet dream for any female that was into the bad boy type. He had that dick game that could drive a weak chic insane. I could understand the infatuation and the mystery that caused the intense attraction. If only he was a fucking mute, then we could have a chance at a real relationship. When he opened his mouth I was reminded that he was only a nigga that wanted to fuck you then fuck up your mind only to see you in public and act like you're a stranger. That was the type of shit that had all these women following his directions and shit. It was crazy that they never wanted to speak up for themselves because, he would take his dick and stroke game somewhere else. That's the difference between me and them, I will always give him his props he was awesome at fucking that was no doubt. It's all the other shit that made me wanna kill his ass.

"Why you keep looking at my ass like that? You want some more huh?" He asked smirking.

That only made me kiss my teeth and roll my eyes. Knowing I couldn't leave this closet without fucking with him some more even a little bit. I walked up to him with a smile on my face. Reaching behind him I was sure to make sure our bare bodies were touching. He bit his lip anticipating that he was going to get some more of my body. Instead I reached behind him snatching one of his button up shirts down.

"I'll just sleep in this one. Thanks for the bomb ass dick show, Champ," I told him with a wink before I turned and walked my ass out of the closet. I heard him kiss his teeth before I left the bedroom.

I don't know what he thought but, us fucking wasn't the start of shit. It was just something that happened and won't happen again. I wasn't looking for a relationship or a fuckship so I hope he was cool with the one closet fuck because that's all I had to give. I knew that this was gonna become a problem down the line though. He wasn't the type of nigga that went along with the program he wanted to call all the shots but, this time he wasn't in control of shit. When I got to the room the first thing I did was hop in the shower again. Once I got out I put lotion on my body then put on his shirt that I took out of his closet. As I slipped it on I could smell his scent all over it. Just by smelling his scent my nipples started to get hard. I kissed my teeth and crawled in the bed. I needed to get out of this house and out of this man's shirt. I eventually dosed off I was stressed and tired so the sleep was definitely welcomed.

"Aye, yo double P. You need to get up. We gotta go," Chaos said waking me up.

I looked up to see him standing beside the bed.

"We don't have anywhere to go. I don't have anything with me no id or anything so where do you think I need to go with you?" I asked clearly showing my irritation.

"Fuck it if you don't wanna eat then don't. Take your ass back to sleep," he said walking back out of the room.

I jumped out of the bed quick as hell.

"Hold up. What am I gonna wear while we go get something to eat?" I asked walking behind him.

"Nah, fam you was just shooting that hot shit. You ain't gotta wear shit cuz, you ain't coming," he said.

"I should've known the asshole was gonna make an appearance. Are you going to bring me something back?" I asked.

"You just called me an asshole but, you need me to do something for you. Picture me doing anything for you. I'm not even gonna bring you a menu," he told me.

I saw his phone on the counter so I went and picked it up. He had me fucked up if he thought I was gonna fold just to get something to eat. I was sure to put the phone on speaker.

"What up?" Toxin answered.

"Bro, can you order me some food and send it to Calamity's house please?" I asked him.

"Who the fuck is Calamity?" He asked.

"You're little friend Chaos. I'm here and he's tryin to be

funny. I can't leave until I get my new id and stuff since he thinks somebody has to beg his ass for something," I said looking directly at him. He gave me a smirk, I gave him a smirk of my own with the middle finger.

"What the hell? What you calling that man names for? From what I hear you need to be thankful that he saved your life," Toxin said sounding amused too amused for me right now.

"Something's wrong with her ass that's all. Sup man, what y'all doing over there?" He asked.

"Ain't doin' shit but, waiting on the kids to go to bed so we can make us one of our own. Jon-Jon and Marsean's kids are here all the damn time I need to put them on my damn taxes," Toxin replied.

"Toxin, I'm the one that called you. I need something to eat and he's not gonna get it. If I had my purse and shit I would order my own food," I fussed.

"Man, don't listen to her I got her. Soon as her shit comes in I'll take her ass home. She gonna make me shake the shit out of her first though," Chaos said laughing.

"Yo, you know how far to go. There ain't no need to share the lines or consequences. Think before you act nigga," Toxin said before ending the call.

"How fucking old are you man? You really called that man about some damn food. I thought you were a damn adult but, you're making childish moves. So damn disappointing. If you want to ride then come on," he said walking to the door.

"I can't go with just a shirt on," I said still walking behind him.

"Why you can't? It ain't like you're getting out. I'm sure that thang is still tired and needs some fresh air anyway. It'll do you both some good," He said with a chuckle.

I slid my feet in a pair of his slides that were by the front door. I know I was looking crazy but, I was hungry too so there. I didn't want to cook so here I was in his passenger seat with a damn button up shirt and some slides. My days were just getting better and better.

❧

Riding in the car with Chaos was like playing with my life. Now the first time I was in the car with him he was driving calm and like he had some sense about himself. Now he has me wondering if my will is up to date enough, if my sister will uphold my wishes after I died from this accident that this nigga was gonna cause. The music was loud and he was zooming in and out of lanes like he had a invisible protective shield around his shit. I kept checking to make sure I had my seat belt on. He had to notice that I was over here scared to death. We got to a stoplight and he stopped at this one. The last two he kept right on going like they didn't just turn red.

"Yo nigga Chaos! I heard some shit about you man," some nigga yelled. Chaos turned the radio down.

"Stop playing with my time man just tell me what you heard," Chaos told him.

"You know it's about that shit that went down at the mall. I'm hearing all types of shit," he said to him shaking his head.

"Whatever you heard that shit is true to the tenth power. Old boy thinking that he got away with some shit but, we all know that ain't true. His time is coming you can bet your next baby mama on that shit," he said and they both started laughing.

"I'm surprised he still breathing," the guy said.

"When you see his ass tell that nigga he better get on his knees every morning and thank the lord and Chaos that he still among the living. He can run but that nigga can't hide forever. He definitely gonna see me though when he least expect it," Chaos said still laughing.

"I don't know what y'all beefing about but, y'all need to settle that shit somewhere else. That shit wasn't cool, for real," the guy said.

"Tell that shit to that man," Chaos said then he pulled off, turning the music back on.

"Chaos," I said speaking loud enough for him to hear me.

"What it do?" He asked turning the music back down.

"Did you have anything to do with what happened at the mall? I'm asking because you made it seem like you just happened to be there like I was," I said to him.

"I was at the mall getting some Jordan's man. It ain't on me that niggas want to act like their about that life when they not. Some niggas wanted to try their hand by coming at me in the mall. I was trying to protect myself when I happened to see you there. I couldn't let you get hurt behind a nigga and his bullshit so I had to make sure you were good. That niggas time will come. You were more important at the moment. Is there anything else you want to know?" He asked.

"So you know who else was in the mall shooting? Is that why you're so pressed about me staying with you? Do you think he'll come after me? How would he even know about me?" I asked.

"I know who the nigga is but, he done got ghost. It's the typical street shit. The only thing is I haven't done shit to this nigga for him to even be coming at me like he is. He's had an issue with me for a while. We all know I ain't hiding from shit so he had to get some weight on his balls before he stopped talking shit behind my back like the bitch he is. He's trying to save face and make a rep for himself by coming at me. Now, that the shit has switched up and I'm looking for his ass he wants to hide. It's straight pussy shit," he told me.

"Who is it?" I asked.

"Nobody for you to be worried about. I only wanted you at the crib until you got your shit back. When you get it then you can bounce. You could even go to Toxin's if you want. I just couldn't have you out here with an x on ya back. You're right though he doesn't know that I have you or that we even know each other," Chaos said.

I looked at him for the rest of the ride. I was enjoying my time with him even though at first I thought it was all for some ass. Shit, maybe I stayed around for some dick. I know my time in house is coming to an end but, I'm not happy about it like I thought I would be.

CHAPTER 10

Chaos

Having her in the house with me wasn't bad because she stayed in that damn room all damn day. We went out to get her a phone so she had to come out for that but, when we came back she was back in there. Toxin kept on texting me asking was either of us dead yet. I don't know why he thought we were over here beefing but, it was quiet as fuck around here. When we fucked in the closet I just figured this is what we were going to do the whole time she was here. I was expecting her to be all up under me and shit. Of course Paradise had to be different she was acting like I had something or that I was holding her hostage. None of that was the case but, when I did try to talk to her she ignored me. I even shot her ass a text a couple of times and she left me on read. Hopefully today would be the day that she would be leaving. I was just waiting on the call for me to go pick up her shit.

I heard her room door open. I continued to look at the TV. Out of the corner of my eye I saw her walk past me and into the kitchen. She was playing with me judging from what she walked her ass out here in she had to be. Another one of my shirts was covering her body. This time instead of letting the shirt hang she had it tied up in a knot on the side. The side where the knot was I could see part of her ass. I could smell my lotion on her. It was some shit that one chic had bought me a while back. The shit smelled manly on me but, on her it made my dick hard. Here it is I was the one that had saved her life, I was also the one that was getting her ID and shit back. Even with all that I was the one that she wasn't fucking with for whatever reason. She had to think that the shit was gonna get to me but, that wasn't gonna happen in this lifetime. She started humming and shit while she moved around the kitchen. Just to drown her out I turned the TV up louder. She stopped humming but, then came the loud banging from the pots and shit she was using.

"Yo, if you don't know how to use them damn things right then leave them shits alone!" I called out to her. She started mumbling and shit, it even seemed like she was slamming them damn pots harder than before.

"Fuck you with your fake saving my life ass," she said loud and clear enough for me to hear her.

That was my opening to talk to her. We were both too damn stubborn to even talk to each other to find out what the problem was. I jumped up and stomped my way into the kitchen. Paradise being Paradise she was standing there waiting on me with her arms across her chest and her head tilted to the side.

"What the hell you just say?" I asked.

"Do you need me to text it to you so you can understand? I know you heard me," she said.

"Nah, I just want you to repeat it now that I'm in your face," I told her.

"Fuck you with your fake saving my life ass. Did you hear that? I would use sign language for the deaf but, I didn't take that class in school," her smart ass said.

"You still breathing ain't you? So how the fuck is me saving your life fake?" I asked as I looked at her breast sitting perfectly under her shirt.

"It was all a set up that's how it was fake," she said sounding crazy as hell.

"What? Where you get that shit from?" I asked.

"From the conversation you had with old boy at the stop light. You weren't just there like the rest of us in the mall. You were the reason for the whole damn episode! Everybody says you don't have a heart but, I thought maybe they were just talking to be heard. Then bam, what do you know, everybody was fucking right about you. You're exactly what everyone thinks you are," she said.

Her voice along with the look on her face was pissing me off more than what she was saying. I had heard all that blah blah shit before. There was always reasons for people to doubt me or act like my rep wasn't really mine. Folks always have something to say when it comes to Chaos. The shit never really bothered me one way or the other but, hearing her say that shit felt different. She wasn't supposed to be looking at me like I was the damn problem right now.

"You really think that?" I asked just to be sure.

"I said the shit didn't I. What the hell am I supposed to think, Chaos? Before we had sex you were so stuck on me staying. After we fuck it's oh you can go stay with Toxin. You used me for sex just like all the other niggas out here," She said looking even more shook up than she did that day.

"Now you're just making up shit in your head to get upset about. How the fuck you come in here starting an argument about some shit we already discussed? I ain't need to do all that just to fuck," I said shaking my head.

"How am I supposed to believe that?" She asked.

"You were never a hostage in here Paradise. You could've bounced whenever you felt like it. Shit you could've walked in here and said you was ready to go and then FUCKING GO. Stop acting like I was holding you here. You're steady worrying about why I told you not to leave when you need to be asking yourself why did you stay. That victim card you're trying to play ain't a good look," I told her.

"See there you go again telling me that I can leave," she told me.

"And here you are still in my face continuing this dumb ass conversation. That's why I don't have a fucking girlfriend or wife because of this bullshit. You're really in here upset as fuck and crying behind some shit you made up in your head. You steady asking why am I keeping you here. When I tell you to leave, you wanna know why I'm telling you to leave. Are you bi-polar or something?" I asked her

She tried to walk away but I stepped in her way. When she went the other way I blocked her again. Walking away wasn't an option right now. There wasn't a guarntee that she would talk to me after she leaves here. That meant that all things had to be said now.

"Talk to me man. You had to know that I was involved some way. I had my fucking gun out when I ran into you. I know you already put two and two together. You can't be mad about that anymore because I didn't lie to you about shit. You never asked and I never said. Since you can't argue about that you want to argue about you still being here but, here you are walking around like you live here. Make that make sense Paradise please?" I asked.

Paradise was standing in front of me but, looking everywhere that I wasn't. Looking all up at the ceiling and shit I could see the water pooling in her eyes. This only made me more confused than I already was. She was on ten and that was too damn much for what she claimed she was mad about. It had to be more.

"You don't get it," she said still looking at the damn ceiling, I think her not looking at me was pissing me off more than anything else right now. Why the fuck couldn't she look at me?

"You're right I don't fucking get it. You're pissed about something you already figured out. Standing here not fucking looking at me like I done did some foul shit to you. I thought we were good so what the fuck is the deal Paradise?" I asked her. I didn't want to scare her but, my patience were wearing thin as hell with this whole scenario.

"You! You turned out to be the heartless motherfucker that everyone says you are. I thought you were different because you chose to save ME that day. You're keeping me here to keep me safe, well that's what I thought. I thought that we were getting somewhere. After we had sex I was thinking that it would be the biggest mistake, but it wasn't. The biggest mistake was me even leaving the mall with you. You're not different, you're the same fucked up ass Chaos that everyone knows. You don't care about shit especially not me. I can't decide on if it was the sex that made you do what you did or the fact that you needed to know if I suspected you were one of the shooters. Which one is it Chaos? Is it both? Do you even know anybody that can get my ID and shit back? If getting the pussy was the real reason then you've succeeded like a mother fucker," she said.

Oh she really was going in on me. This shit had to fucking stop. I was mother fucking Chaos, it was time for her to get off her fucking high horse. She didn't know who she was messing with for real.

"I have about six bitches I could call right now. Have them come over and stand in a fucking line to get the dick. Don't act like you're a fucking prize to have. Pussy is pussy, some are tight some loose but they all serve the same purpose in my book TO GET FUCKED. When I was up in yours I didn't hear you say one time for me to stop but, I'm the bad guy. When I snatched your ass up and got you to safety you may have asked where we were going but, ya black mad ass didn't say you didn't want to go. You think I'm lying about getting your ID and shit well I ain't. Tell you what though, since you're being held hostage and shit. I'll hit them up and tell them to take your shit to your sister and Toxin. You can get a pair of my sweats that are too small and a shirt too. I'm gonna hit Uber's bitch ass up so they can come free the fucking hostage. You can wait here for it or meet them niggas up the block. Either way I'm about to leave so I won't be here and you can leave in peace without the HORRIBLE KIDNAPPER watching over your punk ass. Uber says their faggot ass driver will be here in five minutes, I'm out," I said.

I took my keys off the rack and hauled ass to the car. Getting away from Paradise was the best life decision for me right now. My hands were hurting from wanting to wrap themselves around her neck and squeeze the life from her body. I took a chance stepping out of my usual Chaos ways to help her ass out and the shit she says is how I get repaid. I should've stood behind her ass so she would get hit with a fucking bullet. The crazy part was she was so pressed about what my fucking rep was that she didn't realize I was fucking helping her just to be helping. I didn't want shit from her ass. I was so pissed I wanted to kill some damn body. I didn't have anyone to kill and Rocco's bitch ass still was in the wind. My only way to calm down would be to kill some chic's pussy instead. I pulled over to the side of the road so I could make this call. The phone was ringing too fucking much so that wasn't gonna make her day any better.

"Hello," her ass finally answered.

"Are you home?" I asked.

"Chaos is this you? Yeah I'm home," she said.

"I'll be there in fifteen minutes. I don't need any conversation just some pussy to kill. The shit better be fresh too or else it's gonna be worse," I said ending the call. All these females were about to feel me and they needed to get in line with who the fuck I am.

CHAPTER 11

Paradise

I didn't go to my sister's. I was too much of a mess to go anywhere that I would have to explain why I was pissed about a man being a man. There was a hotel that I always went to when I had to do extra long hours and didn't want to go home. Everyone on the staff knew me well. That was the only place I could think of that I could go to and get a room with no ID or money with me. I even did the makeup for the manager at the front desk for her wedding. Just like I hoped god was on my side at the moment. That manager was the one working the desk when I walked in. It took me no time to get a room key. I know she wanted to ask me what the hell was going on but, she didn't. I didn't feel like talking to anyone about it especially not her. The Uber driver was too scared to fight with me about the change of location. The entire ride over he was looking at me through the rearview mirror. He never asked me if I was okay but, I could see the questions in the way he looked at me. Walking in to the hotel room, I needed a nice hot shower to help me relax. "Why do the one's with the best dick have to be the worst niggas in real life," I said as I got out of the shower.

I didn't bother to look at myself in the bathroom mirror. I had been crying since his ass closed the door. This nigga was not supposed to affect me like this. I was Paradise, no man was gonna have me down and out behind some bullshit. I can't believe I fell for it though. Hook, line, and sinker I was really believing that he was doing for me out of the kindness of his heart. That nigga didn't have a damn heart or a fucking conscious either. Why would I even expect a killer to care about me? The words he told me were playing in my head over and over I needed something to get the words out of my head. I ended up looking at the mini bar of the hotel. Oh well here goes nothing.

What the fuck? Am I drowning? I sat up to see three angry niggas looking back at me. Toxin, Jon-Jon, and Marsean, how did they know I was here? Did I call them?

"You just gonna sit there looking crazy as fuck?" Jon-Jon asked me.

"What are y'all doing here? How did you get in? What the hell is going on?" I asked.

"You're ass needs to go to a fucking AA meeting that's what the hell is going on. How the hell you end up drinking every fucking thing in the minibar but, the fucking water Paradise? That's the first thing you should've drank. Then we get here and you don't have NO FUCKING CLOTHES ON. We look around the room but, guess what. YOU DON'T HAVE SHIT WITH YOU BUT A DAMN PHONE PARADISE!" Toxin yelled.

I had been around my sister and Toxin a lot but, I had never seen this person in front of me right now. I was plotting my escape knowing that my body wasn't going to make it to the door. I was doomed to sit here and take whatever these niggas had in store for me. When he talked about my clothes I looked down to see I had on a full PINK jogging set they even put the furry slippers on my feet.

"Yeah, you had all us in the fucking store buying your drunk ass clothes for you to wear. I don't even shop in that pink ass store for my wife. Leave it up to, motherfucking Paradise," Marsean said.

He was the less upset of the trio. Marsean has always been the quiet one that was why I was low-key scared of his ass.

"Thanks for the clothes," I said to Marsean.

"What the hell you thanking his ass for? I paid for everything," Toxin fussed.

"Thanks Toxin. Are you gonna tell me how you guys ended up in my hotel room?" I asked.

My head was starting to hurt. I need some air. Getting up I went to open the balcony door, just to get some fresh air.

"What kind of dick that nigga walking around with? He got Paradise getting ready to jump behind that shit. I ain't never had no female go that far for the dick," Jon-Jon stupid ass said.

"I'm not jumping I just need some fresh air, jackass," I told him.

"Man all bullshit aside, why the hell are you in here getting all white girl wasted and shit?" Toxin asked.

"I just needed some time to get my mind right. That's all," I lied.

"Okay, so why do it look like you've been crying and shit?" Toxin asked.

"It's just some stuff that I'm going through," I said trying to send him the hint that I didn't want to talk.

"Man, she's fucking lying. She could've went home to get fucking drunk. Broads only go to hotels when they have a place because they don't want to be found. Those are definitely some no good nigga tears that she was crying. I know she wasn't crying because some make-up was discontinued. It ain't hard to figure out all this is behind some nigga and his dick,"Jon-Jon said.

"Why did y'all have to bring him?" I asked shaking my head. This nigga needed a mental evaluation.

Jon-Jon always got on my last nerve. He always had something to say when his ass could just shut the fuck up. Like now, no one needs him to talk and share his fucked up ass thoughts.

"Oh I ain't wanna come but your sister insisted that we all go since we were at the house when you called. Just chalk it up to being in the wrong place at the wrong time," he said making Marsean shake his head.

"Y'all could've left him in the car. My head is starting to hurt and he's making it worse," I said looking at Marsean and Toxin.

"You could've just said no to the dick too. So, what does that mean? You can admit it to us you're suffering from dick depression," Jon-Jon said seriously. Now we were all laughing at this fool.

"Really nigga, there ain't a dick out there that can get me in my feelings," I replied.

"So you're not here because a nigga gave you that deep stroke that fucked your head up so bad that you had to get a hotel room. Then you called your sister got her all upset because you're upset. Now we standing here looking at your hung over ass because you got some 'fuck up my life' dick," Jon-Jon continued.

"You know I hate you right," I told him laughing.

Jon-jon was the fool of the crew. I hadn't figured out if he was the fool on purpose or if that was just how he was. Every time I see him he always has the entire room laughing at some off the wall shit he's said. Most of the time it's something that no one around him has even thought about.

"Not as much as you hate that nigga that gave you that dick," Jon-Jon answered.

"We don't have time for you two to go back and forth all day. What happened? " Toxin asked.

"Chaos pissed me off so I left his house. He's got me all types of fucked up. He can go back to being a creep all he wants because I have absolutely nothing to say to him ever again," I told Toxin. He and Marsean exchanged a look. "I might be hung over but, I ain't blind. What the fuck was that look all about?" I asked.

"You called Ivy and told her that you danced with the devil. I don't know the specifics of what all was said but, you were crying, coughing, and choking on the phone because you danced with the devil. She called Chaos because, he was the last one that you were with. When she asked why would you be crying and shit he said that he didn't know. Chaos said that you two had words but, not so bad that you would be acting out like this," Toxin said.

I sat there staring at him waiting for him to say something else but, he never did. Chaos was carrying it like that well, I got a trick for his ass. Fuck that nigga.

"I'm trying to stay out of whatever you two got going on but, with you calling Ivy I have to get involved," Toxin said.

"I'll call my sister later. She should know that I just need some space when I get like this," I told him.

"If you need me to fuck him up I will, no question," Marsean said.

"Nah, he ain't even worth it. I apologize for her making y'all come check on me. I'm good just need some time to myself. I appreciate y'all though," I said.

"Evidently he's worth something if he has you acting like this don't you think?" Marsean asked.

"No, I could say that y'all should go beat his ass but, just leave it be," I said.

"Y'all need to stop we're all family. Real shit, if you want me to go talk to Chaos I will. He doesn't try us like he does everyone else," Toxin said.

"Nah it's not that important," I told them both.

We talked a little bit more then, they left. I laid across my bed hoping to fall back asleep soon. I decided to scroll through my twitter. I came across a tweet that Chaos had made not too long ago.

@dat_nig_chaos - when these chic's stop thinking their pussy is a fucking super hero the world will be better for us niggas. Ladies always remember when your legs don't open another pair ALWAYS will. I've never been a nigga to scam to get the pussy EVER I dgaf who you think you are? Pussy is always just pussy!

@passionate_paradise - revolving door pussy is all the rage now huh?

@dat_nig_chaos -nah that ain't it, babygirl. I'm just hoping everyone understands that pussy is like weed the shit is plentiful out here. A nigga never has to beg, steal or sneak to get it. I ain't starting today or any other day.

@passionate_paradise -oh it's understood. Have a great life.

@dat_nig_chaos -u too poison paradise

I rolled my eyes at his response. That mother fucker is in the same category as Jon-Jon. Fuck him and all that he stands for.

CHAPTER 12

Chaos

Walking in the house I tossed the keys on the table but, stopped in my tracks when I saw the three of them sitting in my living room like I invited them there.

"Da fuck y'all doing here?" I asked even though I knew why they were there.

"What the hell did you do to that damn girl?" Jon-Jon asked.

"She really sent y'all over here?" I asked laughing at the comedy of this entire situation.

"No, We came because we know it had to be you that fucked her head up," Jon-Jon said.

"Fucked her head up how? I know Ivy said that she had been upset but, she left here after we had words. I don't know how fucked up she is but, I ain't do shit to her. She said some shit, I said some shit, then I left," I said shrugging my shoulders.

"Y'all ain't fuck?" Marsean asked.

"Huh?" I asked. They all looked at each other shaking their heads and shit. If she didn't tell them I beat that cat up then, I wasn't either. "I don't know what the hell y'all talking about," I said looking at them.

"I know she ain't about to jump off the balcony behind some words?" Jon-Jon said.

"Jump? What the hell you mean jump?" I asked.

"Fuck what he talking about. She wasn't about to jump nowhere. I thought you said you weren't gonna take shit there with her," Toxin said.

"The shit wasn't intentional," I told them.

"Since when is fucking not intentional?" Toxin asked.

I know I said I wasn't gonna tell him but, shit. These were the niggas that taught me the game. I couldn't stand here and lie to them like that. Yes, I had done a lot of shit in my day but, lying and hiding ain't in my forte.

"You know how she is. We got to beefing about a shirt or something, right. So bam, all of a sudden she's in my closet throwing all my shit on the floor. I went to grab her and then," I said but was cut off by Jon-Jon.

"Your dick fell in her pussy over and over again," he said shaking his head at me.

"This nigga," Marsean said.

"You know you just complicated shit right?" Toxin asked.

"Nah, I didn't because we both are on the same page now. I ain't fucking with her and she feels the same way about me. We all good and everything is understood," I told them.

Paradise was a chic that I had a one night stand with but, that was it. There wasn't gonna be anything more between us ever. As long as we both understood that then shit was chill in my eyes.

"Did you find Rocco yet?" Toxin asked.

"Hell nah, he's hiding like a motherfucker from me. The thing that confuses the fuck out of me is that he's the one that started all this shit. I don't even know the nigga like that for him to be going at me like he is. There wasn't no fucking reason for him shooting up that damn mall that day. He's a fucking clown for even doing the shit," I told them.

"We all know that nigga is envious as fuck of you," Marsean said.

"Envy ain't a good enough reason for him to be coming at me all hard, this shit is stupid as fuck. People could've lost their lives fucking with this idiot ass nigga but, everybody's thinking it's my fucking fault," I said to them.

"Who thinks that?" Toxin asked.

"Just niggas man," I replied. I wanted to say Paradise's funky ass that's who but, I left it alone. They would've been looking at me all crazy, I didn't need that right now. Paradise was the last thing that should be on my mind but, she was there.

"Yeah, okay. I'm only gonna say this shit once. Stop fucking with Paradise. You did whatever you did and got her all in her feelings, calling Ivy and shit. That only makes Ivy look at me to go fix the shit. This is your last warning the next time I pull up it's gonna be go time. Come on y'all," he told them.

I sat down watching them leave. This shit wasn't supposed to turn out with warnings and shit. I should've asked how the fuck they get in my damn house. Knowing them they broke in, obviously. Paradise is a damn problem that much I do know. There I was again thinking about her. This shit was ridiculous as hell. I had been to fuck two different bitches today and that shit still didn't fix a damn thing. I had nutted more times than I could count today but I was still not relaxed. When I thought about it, I got more upset because I just wasted my energy by fucking with them bitches. I didn't remember their pussy being trash before today but, neither of them did anything for me. This shit was annoying as hell right now. I was about to call another chic to see if shit would turn out the same way it did with the other ones but, I just said fuck it and came home.

Going to my room the first thing I see is the button up shirt she was wearing when she was here. This bitch wasn't even an after thought before all this. Yeah, I loved to look at her when I saw her out somewhere but, she wasn't on my mind like this before. Everything changed when I slid inside her. We weren't fucking with each other on any level any more but, my dick sure wanted to see her ass.

"Are you sure nobody's seen him?" I asked my homie.

I hadn't been out like I wanted to be since Paradise was at the house. Now that she'd left it gave me a lot of time to do what needed to be done. The first thing on the agenda was to find Rocco. He was top priority and he was about to feel my pressure on his ass.

"Nah, that nigga haven't been home either. Where ever he is he has to have shit already there. His mom says he didn't pack or anything when he left the house. She hasn't heard from him since. He didn't even shoot her a text to let her know he was safe. She was acting all worried and shit," he answered.

"Is there a possibility that he's been going in and out through the back door?" I asked.

"I thought about that too. I have Mad Max posted up at his mom's house. He has a perfect view of her back door and a good amount of the alley to get to her backyard too," he said.

I nodded my head, impressed that he had thought of that. Most niggas would do just the basic shit. That's why I fucked with him. He was crazy as fuck but, he was smart.

"Where the hell can this nigga be?" I asked not really looking for an answer.

Rocco hadn't called anyone or seen anyone since before he got the bright idea to shoot up the mall. This nigga should be a damn magician the way he straight disappeared. It pissed me off because I should've had my hands on him by now. I had no clue of how to find him either. Something had to give and quick because I was about to start snapping on everybody if I didn't get my hands on him. I got up and headed to the barbershop. Usually I could find some shit out just by ear hustling. Ace should've heard something by now too. Walking into the barber shop I ended up seeing the one person I wasn't ready to or planning on seeing. I walked past her not even acknowledging her presence. She did the same for me which was cool but, it still felt awkward as hell.

"Oh shit the infamous Chaos is in this bitch," Ace said loud as hell as we shook hands.

"What up man? I needed to get out of the office at the carwash because I was going fucking insane. I'll never understand how those nine to five niggas do it," I told him shaking my head.

"You're not supposed to understand it your a fucking boss out here. You move how you want to move. That's been you for years ain't no changing you now, we all know that much. Are you here for a cut or just to hang out and shoot the shit?" Ace asked.

"Nigga I was just here a few days ago. Your happy clipper ass is gonna have me looking for a new barber if you think every time you see me I need a cut," I told him.

"I'm the only nigga you trust to cut that big ass head of yours. Your threats don't move shit over this way. I'll fuck you up like old boy did," Ace said laughing.

I could see Ace looking from me to Paradise. She must've been staring a hole in my back because his silly ass kept moving his eyes back and forth from me to her. I don't know about anyone else but, I felt the tension in the atmosphere. I didn't have shit to say to her though. I still can't believe she made up a whole fucking scenario in her head just to start an argument and leave. We only fucked once and she was straight acting like a cheating ass wife with the seven year itch. The shit was insane.

CHAPTER 13

Paradise

"Girl, if I just get one time with that fine ass Chaos all you hoes will be hating on me," My hairstylist Lainey said while she was doing my hair.

"Lainey, don't get any of your spit in my hair while you over here drooling over his ass," I said rolling my eyes.

"You can't tell me that Chaos ain't fineee as fuckkkk. Look at his fucking arms bitch. I know he can lift a bitch up and not miss a stroke," she continued laughing.

I was trying not to move too much but, my body was reacting to the memory of the closet sex, the fact that he was here breathing the same air as me, and the fact that I know what his sex was like. She had me wondering why I didn't take the opportunity and have him lift me up while we were fucking. I licked my lips because I was deep in thought and imagining him doing all kinds of things to me. I could hear, see, and feel the memory vividly.

"Can you get me a drink out of the machine?" I asked one of the ladies sitting in the waiting area.

Before it was him staring at me like a creep now here I was

acting like a damn creep. The fact that he was acting like I didn't exist was bothering me but, it was definitely what I asked for. I should just go over there an apologize for how I acted but, that wasn't happening right now. I'm sure he'll do something else for me to be pissed off about.

"Chaos, when are you gonna let me ride you, oops I mean ride out with you?" Some chic said followed by giggles from her and her friends.

"So, you're just letting everybody know you wanna fuck, huh?" He asked.

"We're all grown. I know this is a barbershop/salon but, there ain't no kids in here. I'm sure I'm not the only one thinking about shooting their shot. Why not speak up and say what needs to be said?" She said making herself look more ridiculous.

Chaos got up and started ducking and dodging like he was in a boxing match with someone else. I shook my head because I knew he was about to hurt her feelings. I looked down at my phone praying that my ears wouldn't be hurting to bad after what he was about to say.

"This nigga here," Ace the barber and owner of the shop said with a smile on his face.

"What's all that about?" She asked smiling thinking this was gonna turn out good for her.

"That's me ducking and dodging that tainted ass pussy you're throwing at my ass," he told her.

"I beg your pardon, ain't shit wrong with my pussy. I'm disease free and get checked regularly," she said sounding real proud.

"Something gotta be wrong with it. You're out here pushing pussy like you're the last one out here with it. Then the fact that you're begging me to fuck in a shop full of people lets me know that you don't have a man that cares enough to smack the fuck outta ya silly ass," he said making everyone laugh.

The girl was sitting there like she was stuck on what he had said to her. I just shook my head at the entire scene. She was ready to hop on the dick and throw that ass in a circle a minute ago. However, right now not so much.

"He put that ass in check," Lainey said. I chose not to say anything. "Now she should know better than to come at Chaos like that. He not the type that's impressed by a bold bitch. You not gonna tell me shit; females been throwing pussy at that man since he was younger. That bold shit only pisses him off at this point," Lainey said.

She needed to just shut the hell up. I wanted to get up and walk out but, my hair was half done.

"Aye Paradise when are you gonna let me taste the rainbow?" This dude named Alpha asked. Suddenly all eyes were on me.

"Huh?" I asked.

"You heard me with your sexy ass. You're never with a nigga so damn can a nigga shoot his shot?" Alpha said.

"I never knew if a guy wanted to shoot his shot he asked permission first. Unless telling me that you want to shoot your shot is the way you shoot your shot, I'm not understanding what the problem is here," I told him.

Alpha was what I would consider to be a chocolate pretty boy. He had the dark chocolate skin, pretty straight white teeth, dimples, brown eyes and eye lashes that bitches pay for. He was about six feet at the most. His body was cut due to him being a gym rat, I even heard that he was supposed to be a personal trainer now but, who knows. Besides his smile the sexiest thing about him was his smile and those damn bowed legs of his. I don't know what it was about bowed legs on a man that just put my mind under the gutter. He walked over to the chair I was in. I could feel Chaos staring at me but I was doing a great job of ignoring him.

"What do you want to do when we go out?" He asked as he stood in front of my chair with his hands in his pockets.

"You're the one shooting your shot so you can surprise me on what it is we do while you're shooting your shot," I told him.

He ran his hand down the back of his fresh faded haircut

while he thought about what I said. The way he looked at me gave me chills but, I ain't sure if they were good or bad ones.

"You're not supposed to give the man that kind of control. Fucking with a nigga like me we'll be on a plane to Vegas and you'll come back as my wife on some real shit," he said smiling.

"Oh so we go from shooting the shot to a shotgun wedding. Slow it down man, we can't move too fast you might want to savor the taste and the feeling," I told him. He chuckled a little bit as he looked around the barbershop.

"Some shit I wanna say isn't for the extra listening ears up in here, give me your phone," he said to me.

I passed him my phone, he called his phone with my phone before handing me my phone back. Alpha has a reputation for being a dog ass nigga but, I wasn't looking for a relationship anyway so none of that mattered to me. I don't see nothing wrong with me hanging out with him for a little while.

"Don't do all this in here to put on a show and delete the number when you get out of here," I said laughing.

"I may do a lot of things but, I don't do no acting babygirl, you'll learn that soon enough," he said. He looked me up and down, licked his lips and left out of the shop.

"Bih, that nigga right there is a sexy chocolate god do you hear me. He could damn sure get it," Lainey said.

She continued to talk about the guys in the shop that could 'get it' from her until I was out of her chair. Lainey could finesse the fuck out of some hair but, she could also talk your ass to death while she was doing it. She was good people but, I would never tell her anything that I considered to be a secret that's for sure. After leaving the shop my first stop was to go see my sister. I hadn't seen her in a few days and that's odd for me. We usually see each other every other day and talk to each other a few times a day. I knew she was home because it was the middle of the day and her ass still hasn't gone back to work. She keeps saying she had time to use but, the way she used to work she may have another six months of paid time off. I knocked on the door because, after using the key I had one day and walking in on her and Toxin getting freaky I never walked in unannounced again.

"You're doing the most by making me come open the door for you when you have a key," Ivy complained.

"I'm good on using that key for the rest of my life thanks to you and ya man," I told her making her laugh.

"What you doing here? I thought you had a client today," she said.

"No, I have one the day after tomorrow so I'm just chilling," I told her.

"Oh, some chic brought your stuff here. I was supposed to call you this morning but, I got sidetracked. It's a good thing you came by. Are you gonna tell me what's goin on with you and Chaos?" She asked.

"Nothing to tell. But, guess who's got a date tonight?' I told her.

"Not you I hope. Who the hell are you going on a date with Paradise?" She asked.

"Why you gotta ask me like that?" I didn't like the tone she had with me right now.

"Just the other day you were a full blown alcoholic because of whatever didn't happen between you and Chaos. According to the guys it was really bad. They didn't give me all the details but, even Jon-Jon's joking ass was seriously worried. When I saw that I didn't even want to know what they saw or what was said. I'm just saying maybe you should just chill for a minute before trying to date somebody. Who is this person that you have a date with anyway?" She asked.

"Alpha," I told her.

"Bow-legged Alpha that used to hang with your cousin Rocco?" She asked.

"Yeah, he doesn't hang with Rocco like that anymore," I said to her. She rolled her eyes and kissed her teeth. "Why you gotta do all that?" I asked.

"Paradise you're doing too much. How the hell you go from just living life and doing you to being drunk, ready to jump off a balcony behind a man you claim you don't like? I'm just saying that you look like you're heading for trouble sis. You don't have to put a front on with me. Getting with this new guy who we all know is a dog ass nigga is only gonna end bad. It doesn't matter if y'all don't have sex either before you try to use that to justify it," she told me.

She knew that was gonna be the first thing I was gonna say. Alpha and I were just gonna be friends nothing was gonna come out of this but a few dates.

"It's not that serious," I told her.

"Paradise I know you're grown and all that but, slow down. If you were feeling the way you were feeling behind whatever didn't happen between you and Chaos, you know he was affected. I know Chaos can be an asshole when he wants to but, don't forget he's a man sis. He may not tell you how he feels, shit knowing him he won't but, that doesn't mean he feels nothing. If you start kicking it with Alpha and y'all get close; are you ready to visit him in the hospital?" She asked.

"Hospital for what?" I asked. She only laughed at me and walked away.

CHAPTER 14

Chaos

Watching Paradise try to use Alpha's bitch ass to get to me was fucking laughable. After she did all that screaming and yelling about knowing what I'm about this just proved that she doesn't know shit about me. Once I was done with someone they could be on fire in front of me; I would light a blunt with the flames. I hope she knew what she was getting into by dealing with Alpha's crazy ass. Whatever she was about to get herself into wasn't none of my damn business.

"Yo, is there something you want to tell me, nigga," Ace asked.

I ended up staying with him while he closed the shop and now we were at Malcolm Grand's lounge chilling. This was the ideal spot for when you didn't feel like dealing with the club crowd but, you wanted to go out. We had been here all of ten minutes and this nigga was already ready to question me about Paradise I'm sure. I could tell by the look on his face.

"What man?" I asked even though I already knew what was coming.

"When are you gonna tell me about you and Paradise?" He asked.

"There is no me and Paradise. Guess that means never nigga," I replied.

"Nigga why lie about it. I peeped how you were eye killing her at the shop earlier when she was chopping it up with Alpha. That look didn't say ain't shit going on," he said.

"What the hell brings you two in here?" Malcolm Grand the owner of the lounge we were in said as he stood next to the table.

Malcolm Grand was the oldest of three brothers who made it but was still in the hood from time to time. Their pops was killed when we were younger but, their mom still didn't want to leave the house that they grew up in. His youngest brother Maceo and I were close at one time. I guess you could say that we still are considering we can call each other when needed with no questions asked. It was a lot of history between all of us. I remember when their pops got killed everyone thought that they were going to turn to the streets and shit but, they didn't for the most part. Malcolm and Melvin were older so by the time their pops was taken they didn't have shit to prove. Maceo was the problem child although compared to me the nigga was a saint. His only problem was that he had a temper on him. Once you got him pissed it was gonna be hell to pay before he calmed down. It was the respect that his brothers had that helped keep him out of the gangs. The old heads of the gangs knew that it was essentially on them that their pops had died too. Their pops got killed one night by a nigga looking to join the gang. The murder was a part of his initiation. The fact that he had fucked up in his choice was what got him killed not even a week later. Mr. Grand was the man of the neighborhood that was trying to show knuckleheads the right way to go. He was the local recreation centers coach for basketball and football. He knew a lot of shit that went on in the hood but, never snitched about it. He believed that jails didn't help reform criminals it educated them. When he died it put a huge void in the community.

Malcolm and Marsean were friends so when they would

come around with his brothers we all got to know each other. There were times Maceo and I would end up on the basketball courts in the neighborhood late at night because we were waiting on the old heads to come back from a date or a party somewhere. Being that I was crashing most of the time with Marsean or Toxin I just blended in as one of the boys. Maceo was my homie though over the years we've discussed a bunch of shit that has never been repeated and we both trusted that it wouldn't be.

"Just need to chill out in a non-pussy throwing environment," I told him making us all laugh.

"I can feel that. If you get anything you know it's on the house," Malcolm told us.

"Can I get a bottle of Ace of Spades, some ice, and some glasses?" I asked.

"Damn, big boy style. I see you youngin. Are you sure nothing's on your mind?" Malcolm asked.

"His woman is in here with another nigga," Ace's dumb ass said.

Malcolm looked around as if he knew who to pick out. He looked back at me and smiled.

"What the hell you smiling for?" I asked.

"I know he ain't talking about P?" Malcolm asked moving his eyes to where her and Alpha were sitting.

"This nigga is just as delusional as you," I told Ace.

"Nigga it's all on your face. Every time you turn your head that way you have murder in ya eyes. Let me go get your shit and something to eat. I got a feeling it's gonna be a long night," he said before walking away.

"You know you could go over there and speak," Ace said.

"When did you turn into a messy ass female man? I ain't going to speak to her. She's here with who she wants to be with so I'm good on all of that. Ain't shit popping so just drop the shit," I told him.

He was my man no doubt about it but, he needed to leave this topic alone. I wasn't going over there to talk to her just like she wasn't gonna come talk to me. Shit was all gravy between us as long as we stayed out of each others way. Paradise thought she was gonna make me act out but, that was never gonna happen.

"Here you go fellas. I called the brothers so they're on their way here. Let's get this niggas night out popping. First which one of y'all are driving?" Malcolm asked.

Malcolm didn't play about drunk driving. If you were fucked up in his spot you were going home in an Uber or someone was coming to get you. He nor his employees had no problem cutting niggas off at the bar if they got to leaning.

"I rode with him. We left the shop together after he closed up," I answered.

"Cool, give me ya keys. Y'all will get home one way or another," he said Ace tossed him the keys.

Once Ace tossed his keys to him he turned to look at me. I wasn't up for explaining shit about Paradise to either of them. The way I saw it was all of that was over and done with it. No one needed to know anything about what we did.

"Hey Chaos," some female called out.

I didn't recognize her so I just gave her a head nod. The last thing I needed right now was another female on the roster who didn't know how to deal with getting dick with no attachments. I could feel Paradise staring at me once again. I got my ass up to go to the bathroom. The whole time I was walking I had a feeling that something crazy was about to happen. I wasn't here for bullshit so hopefully my feelings were off because of the alcohol. After taking one of those long piss pauses I flushed and came out of the stall just like any normal person would. When I opened the door to go wash my hands there was Alpha standing there looking dead at my ass. I gave his ass a nod and went to the sink. He was steady looking at me as I washed my hands. Once I cut the water off and dried my hands I looked him in the eye.

"You got something you wanna say?" I asked as I crossed my arms across my chest.

"I don't know what the fuck you and Paradise had going on but, that shit is dead," he said with enough emphasis to instantly make me wanna snap his thick ass neck.

"Alright cool," I said walking past him.

I was trying this new thing called walking away. This was my man's establishment and I did tell him that we were there just to chill. I placed my hand on the door to go back to my table.

"She's with a real nigga now. I don't want no problems with you Chaos," he said with a chuckle.

My hand dropped from the door handle. I was seriously trying to do better just a minute ago. However, this nigga should've just shut the fuck up. I turned around and walked back over to him until we were face to face.

"A real nigga huh? That's what you are?" I asked.

I could see it in his eyes that he was thinking hard as hell trying to figure out what my next move was. He was just so sure of himself a minute ago, now he looked totally different.

"I don't care what she told you. A real nigga should never approach another nigga about his BITCH in a fucking bathroom that's number one. Number two is that before you run up on me behind some drive-thru pussy make sure her pussy ain't wet from seeing me. Since you're a real nigga and all I'll give you a heads up she likes it rough, stupid mother fucker," I told him then I left out of the bathroom.

That nigga better be glad I was trying to keep my word an not fight in here tonight. Paradise was dead ass wrong for whatever she told his ass about me. He was wrong for coming at me in the bathroom. When I got back to the table Maceo and Melvin were there. I sat down with them but, I could see Paradise and old boy were having a heated discussion at their table. From the looks of it she was going in on his ass. I wanted to be petty and go over and ask was everything okay but, as long as he didn't put his hands on her he could live through the night.

CHAPTER 15

Paradise

"Why would you even come out here with that bullshit?" I asked Alpha.

"I'm just saying if you and Chaos had something going on I should know about it. You can tell me the truth, ain't no reason for you to be scared. I'm not gonna put my hands on you," He explained.

I laughed right in his face. Oh yeah, he had a damn problem if he thought I even cared if he had the balls enough to come at me on some Ike and Tina shit.

"Where the hell did you get that shit? How is it that you go in the bathroom completely normal but, you come out all on your angry bird bullshit?" I asked.

I was genuinely confused right now at the fact that he was real life big mad. I had to be missing something right now.

"I'm saying you've been looking at the nigga all fucking night. Then at the shop this morning you two were looking at each other but, trying not to let the other see. I saw him go to the bathroom so I went to holla at him about you," he told me.

"Holla at him about me?" I asked with the stank face. "What would you have to holla at him about, exactly?"

"He needs to understand that we're together now," he said with a serious face.

"Together? We're not together. After this shit I won't have shit else to do with you. Even if we were together there was no reason for you to approach him about a fucking thing. You're doing way to much right now. I haven't said a damn thing about him why would you even approach him?" I wanted to know. Chaos hadn't come up in anything that we discussed so what was his problem with him. There was no reason for him to say more than hi to him.

"I seen the way you've been looking at him and he's been looking at you. I thought I saw it at the shop but, I brushed it off. I couldn't help but see it again. I wanted to know what's up," he said like he had done nothing wrong.

"Why not just ask me? I'm the one you're here on a date with," I asked.

"Bitches lie, simple," he said with a shrug.

Just looking at him pissed me off. I stood to my feet and went full *Love and Hip Hop* on his ass. I tossed what was left of my drink in his face.

"Simple ass motherfucker; how fucking dare you act like this? You talking about we're together nah, motherfucker never that. I wouldn't get with your special ass if you was the last dick on earth. I'm surprised he didn't fuck you up when you approached him behind some bullshit. Niggas get on my damn nerves with this type of bullshit. Fuck you Alpha," I told him as I walked away.

I looked up to see Chaos was one of the people looking at me as I walked outside. I rolled my eyes and kissed my teeth at his ass too. The fact that I actually gave Alpha a real chance made me cringe. This nigga was a whole clown out here. Maybe, I should just go back to how I was before and just leave all niggas alone. It was one bad decision after another.

"Are you good out here?" A male voice asked.

"Hey, Ace, umm yes I'm fine. I have an Uber coming in a few minutes. Thank you for checking on me," I told him with a forced smile.

"I don't know what went on between y'all but, you two should talk," he told me.

"I'm good on Alpha," I told him.

"I'm not talking about Alpha," he told me causing me to turn and look at him.

"Who are you talking about then?"

"Chaos of course; what went on with y'all?" He asked.

What the fuck was it with people tonight? Why was everyone asking about Chaos and I? I hadn't spoken to him since leaving his place and I planned to keep it that way. Just my luck the Uber pulled up. I didn't bother answering him, I just walked away. I opened the door to the Uber only to be pushed inside the car.

"What the hell?" I yelled out.

"Shut up and scoot over P," he said.

My head flew around quick as hell.

"Chaos get the fuck out. Driver can you pull over so he can get out please," I yelled.

"Driver you just do what the fuck you do and drive," Chaos said as he tossed two hundred dollars to the driver.

"Chaos why are you in here?" I asked.

"I had to make sure you were good. What are you doing with that nigga in the first place?" He asked.

"I don't even know now," I answered.

"Tell the truth you were only out with him tonight to piss me off. I know that's what it was so I guess it didn't work out for you. I could tell how his face looked that you didn't tell him about me once I said what I had to say. It's all good that we not kick it or whatever but, if you're gonna go out in public with these motherfuckers make sure it's someone that's halfway worthy. You're out here wasting time and tomorrow isn't promised to either of us, You need to think about that shit harder next time," he told me.

"I know," was all I could say. I could feel him looking at me but, I couldn't look at him right now.

We were in this weird space because of me. He wasn't going to say it but, we both knew it. I realized how wrong I was after I had gotten some rest that night after leaving his place. It didn't help that Toxin called me and gave me a few words. He told me that I was causing unnecessary tension between them. I didn't want to be the cause of anything good or bad. Knowing how long they had been friends is one of the reasons I stepped back completely. I was gonna have to at least be cordial with him even though, deep down I wanted to be so much more.

"You good over there because, you don't look like ?" He asked.

"I want you to fuck me tonight," I said looking at him.

"Huh?" He asked.

"I want you to fuck me similar to how you did in the closet. I admit that sometimes we're like oil and water but, when we're fucking that shit it perfect. I don't know about you but, I haven't experienced anything quite like it before. I haven't fucked anyone else because I know they'll be a waste of time. I need you to bless me. If you want to go back to not speaking afterwards then that's fine but, I need you right now," I told him.

"You're a funny ass chic. So you're telling me you're good with me fucking the shit out of you and acting like I don't in public. Aren't we too old to be sneaking around?" He asked.

"It's not sneaking around. It's scratching each others itch. I don't know if I had the same effect on you but, I can't get what we did out of my head. There's one catch though," I told him. I didn't know if he would agree or not but, this would be a deal breaker for me. I could see that he was waiting for me to continue so I did. "I can be the only one you're fucking in any kind of way,"

"Nah, I can't rock with that. I'm a nigga that needs shit whenever. If I call I need it right then and there. I don't wanna hear no excuses as to why you can't. If you're not working and I call then you gotta make sure you answer the call. Don't get confused when I call I'm gonna wanna fuck no doubt," he told me.

"Same goes for you if I call then you need to make it happen," I told him.

"You're cool with us keeping our arrangement on the low?" He asked. I nodded my head up and down.

"I'm serious," I told him.

The Uber finally stopped.

"Are you coming in?" I asked.

"Are we fucking tonight?" He asked in return.

"Sure," I said with a smile.

"Well, bring your ass then," he said opening the door for me.

Walking into the house the first thing I did was kick off my shoes. I figured since Alpha said we were going to eat that I would wear a pair of the highest heels I had in my closet. Even though I wasn't up on my feet these shoes still hurt the hell out of my feet. I leaned on the back of the sofa and rubbed my feet. Chaos was looking at me licking his lips. He went to get a chair from the dinning room table, placing it in front of me he took my foot in his hand.

"Let me find out you one of those niggas that's into feet," I said to him with a smirk.

"Shut the hell up and enjoy this shit. We all know that nigga wasn't gonna make sure you felt good tonight," he said massaging my feet. It felt so good that I let my head fall back. This was the shit right here.

"Damn, that feels good as shit," I said.

He continued massaging my feet eventually moving up to my calf, then to my thigh. I was just enjoying the massaging he was doing to notice that he had moved the chair all the way up to the back of the sofa. Before I could stop him he had his head between my legs with his tongue moving my thong to the side. It took me by surprise. Although I fully understood that we were going to have sex tonight I still wasn't expecting him to be face deep in my pussy this fast. I reached down and gripped his head.

That only put him in overdrive. He took a hold of my hips and pulled them towards him. I was trying my damnedest to stay up on the back of the couch. The way he was goin in, I was bound to end up on thc floor. While I was trying to maintain balance he slid his finger into my anal cavity.

"Cum Paradise, let me find out this pussy is just as stubborn as the rest of you. You not moving until you cum so make that shit happen stop playing with me," he said.

Before I could answer or even make the first sound of a word he started sucking on my clit like it was a blow pop.

"Ahhhh!" I yelled out at the top of my lungs.

My body jerked as he continued to act as if I wasn't on the verge of dying from convulsing continuously. Instead of holding his head I was now trying to get his mouth as far away from my pussy as I could. He pulled me to him as much as I was pushing his head away. I was certain that he was trying to kill me tonight. I released a sigh of relief when he finally stood up from the chair he was sitting in. I tried to sit up but the look he gave me let me know that I wasn't suppose to move, so I didn't. He kept his eyes on my pussy as he took his pants and boxers off. He licked his lips as he pushed them down to his ankles. He took the rubber out of his pocket, covered himself and entered me.

"Shit," he grunted.

He paused midway during the third stroke. I looked at him wondering what the problem was. He was facing me but, I could tell his mind was somewhere else.

"Chaos," I called his name to get his attention.

"Damn," he said putting his head down. He started back moving in and out of me looking everywhere but, at me. Soon he looked up to the ceiling, bit his bottom lip and made some growling noise I had never heard before. The way he was gripping me turned me on so much that I came all over him and the back of my couch.

Chaos pulled out of me and wobble walked to the bathroom. While he was in the bathroom my doorbell rang. I was confused because there was no reason for anyone to come to my house. It was late as hell and if something was wrong with Ivy she would've called me. I was scared to open the door but, I did anyway. As soon as I seen who was on the other side I knew my night just got a lot longer.

CHAPTER 16

Chaos

While I was in the bathroom I heard her doorbell. It didn't bother me that someone was at her door this damn late. The nigga in me wanted it to be Alpha at the door. I don't know why I wanted him to see me here. It wasn't going to change anything. Paradise and I were still gonna fuck on the regular. He could just be her friend or whatever it was that he was supposed to be to her. I heard the door open but, I didn't hear any voices. I laughed and thanked the lord for shining his light on me. It was obvious that it was a nigga at the door. I stood in the doorway of the bathroom waiting to see if I could hear who it was or what was being said. I couldn't hear a damn thing which meant they were whispering or just not talking. When my mind went to thinking about what they could be doing if they weren't talking I turned the light off in the bathroom and made my way to the part of the house where they were. I turned the corner sure to let her and who ever see that I was fixing my pants. I looked up and smiled.

"Alpha! What up?" I asked giving him a head nod.

"I would shake ya hand but, I just washed my shits," I

told him.

Paradise had a smirk on her face while Alpha was looking confused between the both of us. I was waiting for him to have some more big shit to say like he had to say in the bathroom at the lounge. To my disappointment he didn't have shit to say.

"Chaos," Paradise said.

"Man, I'm bout to leave. I need your car keys though. You know I rode over here in the Uber with you. I can't ask you to drop me off since you got company and shit. Your ass probably don't want to anyway," I told her.

She walked away to go get the keys. I watched her ass boldly as hell. I wish that nigga would say what he had to say. Being that he was straight bitch made he was still on mute. Paradise brought back the keys and handed them to me.

"Don't have your little hoes in my car," she said calling herself being funny. She just didn't know she opened the door for me to say what I wanted to say.

"Don't have no other niggas in my pussy," I told her licking my lips and looking her up and down slow as hell. She was standing there with her mouth open. I turned to look at Alpha who was looking low-key pissed. "Don't be over here too long man. She might fall asleep on you. I know she's tired as hell," I told him as I walked past him to the door. I stopped and turned around to face him again. "Word around town is you got a hand problem. If she don't look like she look now when I see her tomorrow; I'm coming for you," I said before I took my ass out of the door.

Getting to the house I was waiting on my phone to ring with a call from Paradise. When I took a shower and she still hadn't called, I called her.

"Hello," she answered

"Is that nigga still there?" I asked.

"No," she answered sounding irritated but, I didn't care.

"Did he put his hands on you?" I asked.

"No," she answered.

That was all I needed to know I ended the call and took my

ass to bed.

This arrangement that I had with Paradise was working out in my favor. I didn't have to hear her mouth about shit but, this dick going up in her. Even with the little surprise visit she had the other night, she still hadn't brought it up so I didn't either. When I picked her up the next morning we exchanged good mornings and that was it. If we were on something other than just us fucking things would be totally different. I would've fucked her and him up, she would be all in my ear fussing about the shit I said. However, since we weren't on that shit was all gravy between us.

She was a great distraction from the fact that I found out Rocco's mother had put out a missing person's report on him. I guess she wasn't lying when she said she didn't know where he was. I still had someone watching her house though because, for all I knew it could be a game to try to make it look like his ass was missing when he wasn't. I had been looking everywhere for his ass but, coming up with nothing. I was riding out for a little while so I decided to go check on Toxin because I hadn't heard from his ass in a while. I needed to get out and get some air so his place was my first stop. When I got to the door the one person I wasn't expecting opened the door.

"Chaos, nice to see you," she said.

"What it do Paradise? Is Toxin here?" I asked. She didn't answer but, she stepped to the side allowing me to step into the house.

"He's in his man room," she said as she sat back down on the couch in the living room.

I was checking out what she had on and she had all her damn stomach out. I wanted to play with her navel ring with my tongue like I had done last night. I licked my lips and refocused by attention to go down to the man cave. Toxin was down there watching a basketball game.

"What up old head?" I said slapping hands with him and taking a seat on the couch beside him.

"What it do?" He asked.

I could feel the bullshit about to come. I wasn't for the shit today. So instead of waiting for him to get to the point I asked his ass about it.

"What the hell is on ya mind man? You got something you wanna know?" I asked looking at him.

Toxin was one of the niggas that I looked up to but, this shit with how he was carrying me about Paradise was getting on my fucking nerves. I let him have it the last time but, that was the only pass he was getting from me. He didn't need to be all uptight about it any fucking way. Paradise was grown as hell.

"I was out your way the other night," he said not looking at me.

"Okay, and you didn't stop by?" I asked.

"Nah, I pulled up to the crib and shit. I even used the key I got because I thought maybe your ass was sleep or something. You were in the room but, you weren't sleep. You were in there fucking Paradise though," he said looking at me.

"When the hell did you get a key to my spot?" I asked.

I didn't give his ass a key so I needed to know how the hell that shit happened.

"I called up one of my locksmith friends and they made a key for me. That's how we got in ya shit the last time we were there. When we talked to you about fucking with Paradise," he said finally looking at me on that last part.

I tried to hold it but, I couldn't I laughed right in his face. I know he didn't think he was punking me or some shit. The thought of what he was trying to do was hilarious to me.

"Man look, the last time we talked her and I both were on some fuck you shit. We talked about everything and now we just on some fuck me good shit," I said laughing. He didn't think it was funny because, he wasn't laughing with me.

"Ain't shit funny," he said trying to keep playing this daddy role.

"Nah, it ain't funny how you trying to play me behind a grown ass woman. We are both on some let's fuck type of shit. I'm positive that I'm not the first nigga to get up in her. She's the one that proposed the arrangement in the first place. You're in here trying to dictate how her pussy moves while she sending me pictures and videos of the motherfucker. That don't make a bit of sense to me. How you tracking a pussy that clearly is attracted to my black ass dick?" I asked him.

I know I could've used better words but, the shit was, what it was. He was straight acting like an asshole about some shit that had nothing to do with him or anybody else for that matter. If he was gonna keep coming at me behind her he wasn't gonna like the shit to come out of my mouth.

"This shit just seems like a big mistake to me," he said.

"If it is a mistake then it's one that her and I are going to have to make. Honestly I don't see us stopping no time soon. Matter of fact when I leave here I'm gonna text her ass to see who spot we need to meet up at. We may not know how to have a civilized conversation with each other but, we got this fucking shit down to a fucking science," I said laughing at the word play I used.

"Don't play with her man," he told me.

"I get what you saying but, she's the one you need to be checking. She got the pussy that will make me fuck around and kill her ass," I told him.

"That shit must run in the family," he said shaking his head. We both had no choice but to laugh. I hoped this was the last time we had this bullshit ass talk.

"What did you and Toxin talk about earlier?" Paradise asked me.

We were sitting up in her bedroom looking at television now. We had just gotten done fucking each others brains out. It had become our routine to hook up fuck, take a break, fuck, take a break, then fuck some more. Quickies weren't something that we did. It always took hours for us to get our fill of each other then we would part ways and do it all again in a couple of days. We never talked about shit that mattered though. It was always something basic or just sports.

"There ain't no need to switch shit up now. If you wanna know what we talked about ask him," I told her.

"So you can fuck me but, we can't talk?" She asked. I could tell by her tone that this wasn't gonna go good at all.

"We didn't agree to talking and getting to know each other we agreed to fucking," I told her.

"Wow, well since we're not fucking. I guess I should go," she said getting off the bed.

I knew she wanted me to say something but, that shit wasn't in me. She started mumbling and stomping around the room. I just turned the TV up on her ass. She left out of the house making sure to slam the door. I couldn't be who I was if I didn't hit her ass up with a text.

Me: I'll give you a couple of days to chill out but our deal still stands wit yo mad ass

Poison Pussy: kiss my ass Chaos

Me: soon as you bring it back over here I will

I tossed the phone on the bed because I knew her ass wasn't gonna hit me back. She could play mad all she wanted to but, I was gonna have to roll up on her ass if she tried to buck about our deal. She better put those emotions to the side or better yet ride this dick like she's mad at it. Just the thought of her doing that made my dick jump. I needed to get my ass up and go do something besides think about fucking Paradise. So I guess I would be hitting up the club tonight. I sent a text out to hit up the fellas to let them know I was heading out tonight. It was all about booze and bitches tonight.

CHAPTER 17

Paradise

"Chile did you see Chaos with his fine ass sitting in VIP with his boys. All of them could get it. Just call me Choo-choo because they could run a fine nigga train on me," Sasha, Porche's sister said.

I just sat there sipping my margarita as her and her friend slapped hands. They were the poster children for all the ghetto birds in the entire world. I shook my head at how much they celebrated the fact that they just agreed that they would let a group of niggas run a train on them. Some females just didn't care about a damn thing they said or did.

"What's the matter P? You've been quiet all night," Porche asked.

"Nothing," I lied rolling my eyes.

When she called saying that we needed to go out because we hadn't been out in a while. The last thing I expected was for her to bring the hoe squad with her when she picked me up. I needed to get out of the house though. I was tired of sitting there thinking about all the things I had done sexually with a nigga that I had no claim to. The way we fucked you would think we were in love, married for ten years and working on kids. Instead of all that we were just fucking.

“I know that look. You’ve been working too hard. Let’s find you a new boo,” Porche said.

“She needs some dick,” Sasha said.

“You’re funny. Don’t worry about my pussy movement. Just keep passing yours out like it’s a piece of candy,” I told her with a smile.

“Not tonight ladies! Tonight we’re going to drink and have fun no arguing,” Porche said as she danced around.

Porche never liked it when me and her sister argued. I felt about her sister exactly how Ivy felt about Porche. The only difference was that Ivy didn’t hang around us unless she absolutely had too. Porche was always bringing her sister along with us. Every time Sasha would say something letting us know how much of a hoe she was. Most of the time I spoke up, pulling her card. She got under my skin for whatever reason. I watched as one of the bouncers came over to the table and whispered in Porche’s ear. She looked at him, glanced up to the VIP section that Chaos and the rest of the hood niggas were, and smiled.

“Ladies, tonight is our night. We’ve just been asked to accompany the gentlemen in VIP,” she said with an even bigger smile.

My stomach dropped to the floor. It was bad enough that Chaos and I were in the same club together. I didn’t need to be in the same section with his ass. It didn’t help that Alpha was here too. This night was just getting better and better. Soon as we got to the section Sasha hopped her hot pocket pussy ass on the couch with Chaos. I rolled my eyes and kept my thoughts to myself. I quietly sat down on one of the other couches. The section was so big that all the couches weren’t facing each other. That was a blessing for me because I didn’t have to sit and watch Sasha throw herself at Chaos.

“Why you over here with ya man entertaining other bitches?” Alpha asked as he sat down.

"I'm not a bitch, and he ain't my man," I told him.

"It damn sure didn't look that way to me. It would be a shame if he was because then you would have to choose between dick and family," he said then he stood to his feet like he was about to walk away but, I had a question of my own first.

"Why are you even in this section? It ain't like y'all rock like that. The last I knew you two didn't even hang together. You have to be here just to start some shit," I told him.

"Don't worry about it your man ain't in danger tonight," Alpha said with a smirk on his face.

"Why the hell are you being so damn weird tonight? You're looking spaced the fuck out and you're saying shit that doesn't make sense. Alpha maybe you should go home," I expressed to him.

I didn't know what the hell he was talking about. Why would I have to choose between dick and family? I poured myself another drink of whatever bottle that was on the table. I wasn't going to worry about that babble that Alpha was spitting. He must be just as drunk and high as the rest of the niggas in here. Since Chaos was entertaining company on the couch I decided to go to the bathroom. Making my way through the maze of people to the bathroom. I got a bad feeling in the pit of my stomach. It was one of those feelings that something wasn't right but, you didn't know what the something was. I looked around and didn't see anything out of the ordinary. Shrugging it off I walked into the bathroom. I didn't have to pee or anything I just need a few minutes to catch my breath without hearing Sasha giggle all loud to whatever bullshit Chaos was spitting in her ear. I was fixing my hair and wiping the beads of sweat off my forehead when the door to the bathroom slammed shut.

"Alpha what the fuck are you doing in here?" I asked backing up grabbing my clutch bag.

"I came to get what's due to me," he said walking toward me.

"What the fuck are you talking about?" I asked.

"Rocco told me that you'd let me fuck," he said rubbing his hands together.

I felt around in my bag for the plastic nail file I always brought with me to the club. I knew I couldn't get a gun past the metal detectors so I brought the file with me. It was plastic but sharp enough to stab a nigga if I had to.

"Rocco? I don't even fuck with that nigga. I don't know what kind of deal y'all worked out but, I ain't fucking you! If you come any closer I'm gonna stab the fuck out ya eyeball," I told him. I still had my hand inside my bag so he didn't know what I had in my hand.

The door was kicked open and I saw Chaos and few other guys jump on Alpha. I was standing against the wall too shook up to move as they beat him until blood was all on the floor. It was the wildest shit I had ever seen but, I couldn't look away. The other guys were now trying to stop Chaos from killing Alpha.

"Chaos!" I screamed and everyone stopped including him.

"Did he fucking touch you?!" He yelled at me. I was so shook by everything including the way he was screaming at me. I shook my head from side to side. "Get your shit and let's go!" He yelled. I moved around as best I could in the bathroom. "Move the fuck out of her way. Paradise go to my car," I heard him yell.

I kept walking even though I didn't know exactly where his car was. As I walked to the door it was as if the crowd parted like the red sea. I kept my head down but I could see everyones feet moving out of my way as I came through.

"What happen P?" Porche came up to me. I was about to tell her when I heard Chaos coming up behind me.

''I thought I told you to go to my car," he said until he was standing behind me all possessive and shit.

"Chaos, I didn't know you and Paradise were close?" Sasha said.

"Why you still in here?" Chaos asked me ignoring Sasha's question.

"I stopped to talk to them for a minute," I answered.

"Don't y'all have her phone number? You can call them they can call you. I thought y'all females always went to the bathroom in pairs or groups when you came to the club. Why the fuck was she alone?" He asked while looking at Sasha, her hoe friend and Porche.

"I didn't know she left from the section. She didn't tell us," Porche answered.

"She ain't spoke to me all night but, I peeped when she got her ass up," he said shaking his head.

"I thought we were gonna leave tonight together, so we can have some fun back at your place," Sasha said stepping closer to him. He took a few steps back to stay a good distance away from her.

"Don't walk up on me with ya shitty talking ass," Chaos said.

I noticed how he kept his hand around my waist as we stood in front of them. He was still in protect mode even if it was just Porsche and the girls. Even when I tried to step away he was sure to grip me tighter.

"You wasn't just saying that," Sasha said.

"I was only whispering all that bullshit in your ear because I ain't want you to look at me when you talked. Like, I was saying if she's y'all homegirl ain't no way she should've been in the bathroom alone. Y'all better be glad I got there in time or y'all bitch asses would be on my get fucked up list too. You saying you didn't see her leave is bullshit. I peeped it and went to go check on her and we're just," Chaos was about to spill all the beans but, I stopped him.

"Come on Chaos or I could just call Toxin to come get me," I said. He stopped talking and looked at me.

"Yeah okay, keep fucking playing with me Paradise," he told me.

He ushered me out of the door of the club. I waved bye to the girls and got in his car. I don't know how his car was out front waiting on us but it was. He made sure I was in and my seat belt was on before he went to get in the driver's seat.

"You need to leave those birds alone. Everybody ain't your damn friend. If I wasn't there you could've got fucked up tonight. I don't trust those hoes," he said before pulling off like a bat out of hell.

CHAPTER 18

Chaos

I stood by the bathroom door listening to her cry while she was in the shower. I was going to take her to Toxin's house but, decided to bring her to my condo instead. It was closer to the club and nobody would bother her here. I wanted to leave and go kill Alpha. What the fuck was that nigga thinking? There's no way he could've thought he could get away with the shit he just pulled. She was taking too long to come out of the bathroom. I walked up in there to see her standing in the corner of the shower balling. Seeing her like that hurt my heart. A nigga like me didn't even know I had a heart. I was a killer; a nigga that most feared in the streets. I kicked my shoes off, took my pants and shirt off and got in the shower with her. I pulled her into my arms and just held her as she cried. I didn't know what else to do with her right now. I waited until her tears calmed down enough before I started washing her body. This was foreign territory for me but, I knew I couldn't leave her alone. After drying her off I gave her one of my wife beaters for her to sleep in.

"Are you hungry?" I asked her.

"No but, you know you can call Toxin to come get me. I don't want to be in your way," she said.

I know she wasn't trying to but, she damn sure had pissed me off.

"Aye, for real I get that Toxin is your brother-in-law and all that but, stop telling me to call that nigga. I'm not trying to say that I think there's something going on with y'all because I know the truth. I hope you don't take this shit the wrong way and all. You calling on him all the time has got him thinking he's more than a brother-in-law. He treats you like you're one of his kids and this is the reason why. I understand you don't like to get your parents involved and all that but, you've got me now. So fall the fuck back with all that call Toxin shit because I ain't calling his ass. You better not call him to come rescue you from shit else either. My number is in your phone just like his is. Call me and not him from now on," I told her.

"Chaos, I understand but, I can't call you. We're just fucking remember. No conversation right? Ain't that what you said?" She asked.

"Paradise look just call me man damn. Why you gotta be so damn difficult all the fucking time? Just call me period. If I find out you called him instead I'm gonna fuck you like I hate your ass," I told her.

"Okay, you don't have to say it like that," she told me.

It was a shame that me talking to her crazy was the only way she understood what the hell I was saying. Her ass was worse than the hood kids in the neighborhood. They just stood there and looked at you crazy if you asked them nicely to come here. They would come running if you throw some curse words in there though. That's how I had to do Paradise most of the time.

"I hope you understand what I'm saying," I told her.

"i got it but, what you just said takes us out of the just fucking category," she said.

"Technically we were out of that when I fucked up Alpha in that bathroom. You don't have to tell me what happen before I got there. You said he didn't get to touch you so I'm good with that. Now, if you need someone to talk to about it then call me or your sister. I'll listen and help you any way that I can," I told her.

I knew that she was aware of who would be in her corner when she needed them to be. I just wanted her to know that my name belongs at the top of that list.

"You just described all boyfriend actions, Chaos. That is not what this is," she told me.

"Ain't nobody said shit about what you talking about. All I said was don't call Toxin just call me. How you get all that other shit out of that is beyond me? I know what we are ain't shit gonna change. You need to stop leaning on that man so much. I know Ivy ain't gonna let nothing happen to you so that brings Toxin into the equation. You gotta stop calling on him so much. Any woman out here fucking a nigga on the regular should be able to call his ass if she needs some help with whatever," I explained.

She started laughing loud as hell. I shook my head at her but, I was glad to see her laughing instead of crying. I laughed with her. She laid her head on my shoulder and that's when it hit me that shit was indeed changing for us. I didn't really want it to change because with changes came complications. What we had going was good just like it was but, I had a feeling shit was about to get sideways. I just didn't know how bad it was going to get.

I waited for her to fall asleep before I eased out of the bed. I left the door open so I could see if she turned the light on or anything. Once I was seated at the desk in the room across from my bedroom I made a phone call.

"Yo, I saw ya messages. I just got her to sleep so what's the deal?" I asked Spoke, one of the fellas that I had put on snatching Alpha up.

"What do you know about Paradise? I'm saying we all came up in the same hood and shit but, man. I don't know how true this shit is but, Alpha is saying that she's old boys cousin," he told me.

"Who's cousin? Stop talking in circles," I told him.

"Rocco, she's Rocco's cousin. Did you know that?" He asked.

"You sure that's what Alpha said. How come nobody knew that shit?" I asked.

The shit just sounded a little too convenient to me. If they were cousins why the hell none of us knew. I know damn well Toxin didn't know because he would've said something way before this shit went this far with him and I. I stood to my feet and started pacing back and forth. Spoke was talking but, I wasn't listening to shit he had to say. I was going over in my mind to see if I had even seen her and Rocco in the same place. Shit, that nigga didn't even come to the birthday party Toxin had for Ivy. If they were cousins why wasn't he around? I got Spoke off the phone and called Toxin.

"Yo," Toxin answered.

"Did you know your wife was Rocco's cousin?" I asked getting to the point.

"Nah but, hold up," he told me. I heard him moving through the house opening and closing doors. "Ivy, y'all got a cousin named Rocco?" I heard him ask.

"Yeah, why?" She asked.

"Why I haven't met this nigga?" He countered.

"Because I don't fuck with them. Him and his bitch ass mama, which is my mother's sister, are some hating ass mother-fuckers. We're only related by blood. Paradise was the only one going to check on them until a month or two ago. She went over there an of course Auntie got to talking crazy about my mama so she cursed her out and left. I doubt if she's even talked to Rocco. Are you gonna tell me why you coming in here randomly asking about my relatives?" She asked.

"Just know that the mother fucker is bad news. Stay the fuck away from him. If he calls or pops up let me know right then. I don't care what we have going on," he told her.

"Okay, you still haven't told me why yet?" She said I chuckled at how much her and Paradise sounded alike when they got pissed or irritated.

"He's donc some fucked up shit in the streets. I'm not playing stay the fuck away from his ass," he told her again. I heard a door close and him mumbling to himself.

"Yo, Toxin are you good over there nigga?" I asked.

"Hell nah, how the fuck I ain't know that? This shit is gonna complicate every fucking thing. How did you find out?" He asked.

I gave him the run down on everything that went on tonight finishing off with what Spoke had told me. He got a little too quiet on me.

"You still there?" I asked.

"I'm here trying to piece shit together. Did Spoke find out why Alpha tried Paradise like that tonight? He had to know something was up with y'all after he saw you at her place. It doesn't make sense for him to not heed your warning. Shit is off man there's something we're not picking up on," Toxin said.

"You might be right. Let me sleep on it. Then we can go check out Alpha our selves to find out if we can figure this shit out," I told him.

When I got back in the room my mind was going a mile a minute. I watched Paradise sleep. She seems so innocent while she sleeping. Too bad she had to wake up and talk. I thought to myself laughing. She wasn't supposed to be in my life like this. Yet, here she was in my bed. On top of that she was some kin to the one nigga I dreamed of killing. We were going to have to talk about that in the morning. I know that Ivy said that they don't fuck with Rocco like that but, sometimes that beefing shit goes out of the window when he turns up dead.

CHAPTER 19

Paradise

I was tired of having to be saved and getting saved by Chaos. How is it that he's always there to save my ass? It wasn't that I wasn't grateful but, I just was stuck on trying to figure out why Chaos? It was as if there was some force that was pulling us together. Instead of talking to him about what happened in that bathroom, I left his condo early this morning while he was still sleeping. I called my sister and talked to her about everything before taking a shower in my own bathroom and getting in my own bed. I slept good as hell but, I'm sure that was because of the melatonin that I took. I actually had a client to do today so I got up ready to get busy and not think about all the other shit that was going on around me. I was sure to send my cousin Rocco a nice long text to let him know I was gonna kick his ass when I saw him. I didn't bother to call his mama because all she was gonna do was tell me she didn't know where he was and how Alpha could've been lying. Not wanting to hear her bullshit I called his ass. He didn't pick up the six times that I had called so I left the text.

Walking into the photo studio with a smile on my face and

my make-up suitcase ready to work was the only thing that gave me peace. This was the only sure thing in my life right now.

"Hey Paradise, you look gorgeous as always. I just love your melanin," Scott the photographer said.

Scott had a thing for black women. He called us 'melanin queens' no matter who you were. He and I would flirt here and there but, we would never go further than that. I wanted my work to propel me to the big photoshoots not my pussy. I stayed away from doing more than flirting on the job.

"Thank you Scott, where is Marisa?" I asked.

"She's in her dressing room. You know she's in there burning sage like the shit is going to change her mood," he said rolling his eyes.

I took a deep breath and headed to her dressing room. Marisa Monroe was a woman who's status in life was well below the status she thought she was in her head. She was a socialite that had a strong following on every social media platform that there was. Due to her heavy following she had a few deals with all types of brands to wear and/or promote their products on her pages. Today she was doing a photoshoot wearing some athletic brands clothing and foot wear. Instead of taking a selfie with her latest iPhone she insisted on having a professional shoot with all the bells and whistles just for the pictures to be posted and circulated through the internet. I admit most of the time a selfie would do but, I understand her reasoning for today's shoot. There were two racks of clothes and a row of about twenty pairs of shoes against the wall in her dressing room.

"Hey Marisa are you ready?" I asked.

"Oh Paradise, I'm ready but, the one thing that's bothering me is will I have the look I've actually been working out. You know what I mean the tired look. Is there a way that you can make me look tired with the magic suitcase that you have?" She asked me.

"I'm sure with what I have and some light movement we can make you look tired. Are you sure that's the look that the company is going for?" I asked.

"I don't know they always let me go with whatever look that I choose. I'm just tired of always being dressed to the nines and having my face beat to the gods. I was looking at my profiles on the way over here it seems like I'm losing my down home look. I don't want to become just another influencer that's lost touch with the people that she's influencing. It's hard for me to explain but, I hope you're getting it," she told me.

I looked at her confused because today she seems more down to earth than ever before. Looking around I didn't see the usual which is various alcoholic beverages scattered on the vanity. Today there was a few tea bags and empty water bottles. Something was up with her definitely.

"Are you okay?" I asked.

"Yeah, well, no I'm not but, we can get this shoot over with. Life has a way of making you face things you never thought you would see. I'm not going to lie to you Paradise. My body's here but, my mind is back home. My dad had a heart attack this morning while I was in the shower. When I got out my mom had left me six messages of her screaming and crying on the phone. I still haven't called her back. I don't know what to say or do right now. I left my phone home because I knew she wasn't going to stop calling," she told me with a few tears falling.

"Why didn't you call her back? I don't even understand why you're here right now," I told her.

If something were to happen to my parents or my sister I wouldn't be here. They would just have to figure things out without me. They were my everything, I can't imagine them hurting and me not being by their side. Even with my parents not being together anymore I would always be there for them just like they had always been there for me.

"My family and I don't get along like most families. They think that I've forgotten them now that I'm doing all this fancy stuff. Eventually I just stopped going around them because every time I did my parents would badger me about getting a real job and not 'selling sex' as my dad put it. Paradise I haven't seen my parents or my siblings in four years. They stay no more than an half an hour away and it's been four years," she cried.

Now I understood why she wanted the tired look. She needed it to express the grief and worry that she was going through without hurting the campaign. I knew what I needed to do for her.

"Come on let's get to work. The quicker we get this done; the quicker you can go be with your family. I know it's gonna be hard but, you have to be there with and for them," I told her as I wiped her face.

"I'll go, I promise, I'll go," she told me.

She turned around in her chair and started drying her tears while I started getting my makeup out of my bag. This was going to be either really good or really bad. I prayed that it would turn out to her liking though. Once I got the things that I needed to get started I turned and looked at her.

"Are you ready to slay this photo shoot?" I asked.

"I'm in your hands Paradise," she said with a forced smile.

❧

"Oh my god Paradise these turned out just the way I wanted them to. I can't believe you guys pulled this off. These look great I look tired and fabulous all at the same time. This is perfect," Marisa cheered as we looked at the photos on the computer screen.

She was right there wasn't a bad shot on the screen. I didn't want to toot my own horn but, I did that shit.

"They look great," Scott added his two cents in.

"Thanks y'all. We did this together, it wasn't just me," I told them.

"Once these hit the internet everyone is going to be wanting to know who did my makeup. I hope your ready for the glow up," Marisa said with a smile and a hug.

"This photo shoot is a rap. Don't you have somewhere to be," I said to Marisa.

"I'm going I swear," she told me as she walked back to her dressing room.

I pulled my suitcase back to my car. I rolled my eyes at the black on black range rover that was parked far enough away to not look suspicious. I knew they were there under Chaos' orders. Rolling my eyes because, I knew that me telling him that I would be fine wasn't going to convince him to get them off me. I first noticed them when I came out of the house this morning. The thought of calling Chaos crossed my mind but, he was going to want to talk about t happened with Alpha at the club. I didn't want to talk about that shit right now and especially not with Chaos. I wasn't in the car good when my mother called.

"Yes mother," I answered.

"Don't try that yes mother shit with me. I have to call you so you can come over," she said making me smile.

"No," I answered.

"So why the hell am I doing it then," was her reply.

"I'll be there in a minute. I'm just leaving a photo shoot," I told her. I was a little thrown off when she ended the call without saying goodbye or that she loved me. I brushed it off and started the car. I hope she cooked because I was bringing my appetite along with my ass.

CHAPTER 20

Rocco

"Is she on her way?" I asked Auntie Renee.

"Yeah, she's on her way. She just left a photo shoot," she answered.

"There you go with that bullshit. You didn't have to add that photo shoot shit in there. Who the fuck cared that she was a photo shoot. She was probably holding the lights or something," my mama said making me laugh.

"One of these days all that hate is gonna get your ass killed," Auntie Renee said to me and my mother.

"Let me guess are you gonna kill me? You would kill your own sister?" My mama asked.

"Shit your ass is already dead inside. What's gonna be the difference, Gail?" Auntie Renee asked my mother.

"Y'all cut all that arguing out. It's giving me a headache. Y'all not really talking about nothing anyway," I told them both.

"Why you so mad with my girls?" Auntie Renee asked me.

"They think they're all that because they're with those niggas Toxin and Chaos. Toxin's not as bad as Chaos, I really don't have no beef with him. That nigga Chaos is gonna make me kill him though. I didn't even know that he was fucking with my family. At first I was mad that P would get with the one nigga I hate. Then I thought about it, I can use that shit to my advantage. I called up mama to see if she wanted to come ride and here we are," I told her.

"Chaos? I haven't met him. Now Toxin, that's my son-in-law," Auntie Renee said all proud.

Seeing her talk about that nigga Toxin like that made me want slap her ass. If she wasn't my auntie I would've, yeah I was here on some disloyal shit but, her daughters started it. If they would just get with niggas that I didn't have a problem with then we would be cool. Paradise may not have known what was going on with Chaos and I but, she had to know now. If she would've kept talking to Alpha she wouldn't be in this. Now she's mixed up in street shit and she has her nigga to thank for that. The door opened and in walked the woman of the hour.

"What's up cousin?" I said with a smile.

"What the hell is going on here? Mama are you okay?" Paradise asked looking at Auntie Renee.

"She's fine ain't no body here to hurt either of y'all. Rocco has some questions for your disloyal to the family ass," my mama said.

"Disloyal to the family?" Paradise asked looking between my mother and I. "The same family that proudly told Alpha that I would fuck him. Rocco ain't loyal to nobody but, his damn self. Both of y'all need to get out of my mama's house,"

"This is my sisters house little girl. We're gonna talk about this like a real family should," my mama said.

"Is a REAL family coming over here? We haven't been a real family in years. I was the only one coming to check on y'all until I came over there and y'all pissed me off. You two are the most hating ass people I know. Tell me why y'all are here," Paradise said.

"Chaos," I said watching her reaction closely.

She was trying to act like me saying his name wasn't bothering her but, I could see the worry in her eyes. Shifting her stance she looked around.

"What about him?" Paradise asked.

"He and I have some things to discuss. I need you to get him here," I told her. Paradise just laughed at me shaking her head.

"No," Paradise told me. I was hurt because I was at least expecting her to think about it. I was family but here she was choosing some nigga she didn't even know over her family. "How the fuck you choosing a nigga that you just started fucking over your family? That nigga don't give a fuck about you. I don't know what kind of game he spit to you but, believe me it was all bullshit just to get the pussy," I told her.

"Why did he do all that when he could've just asked you for my pussy like Alpha did?" Paradise said with a smirk on her face.

"I never told Alpha that shit you can stop saying it. He was fucking lying. I would never do that to family," I told her.

"Says the nigga that's trying to get me to help him set a nigga up," Paradise replied.

This wasn't going the way I wanted it to. We were supposed to get her here and Paradise was supposed to call that nigga Chaos. It was supposed to be a done deal no pushback from her or her mama. She needed to get with the program and quick. I knew I was running out of time. I had to either get him here or get low again.

"That nigga ain't nothing but a piece of dick. You can get that anywhere. I heard that thick pieces of chocolate were in right now," my mama said smiling.

"I should slap the fuck out of you right now. You damn right it's in and it's been in, I thought you knew. Charlie knew what the fuck the deal was and that was years ago," Auntie Renee said.

"Wait a minute, what is she talking about?" I asked my mama.

"Nothing she just wants to start shit," my mama said but she looked shook.

"Tell him how the man you kept flaunting around the family is the same man that left your ass high and dry for this dark chocolate. Just tell the truth and tell them that's the real reason you don't like my ass. You can't stand that the man you were crushing on in junior high school and went on a few dates with turned out to be the love of my life and my daughters father. You've been hating me for a long time but, I never told anyone why. Todays the day that all this shit come to a head. You hated my girls because you thought I stole your man from you. Newsflash, he was never yours. You were too fucking hurt to realize that shit. You brought your ass over here trying to get on my damn child about some dick when you clearly let some dick that you never had break up the family," Auntie said standing to her feet.

The room was quiet as hell, all eyes were on my mama. I was speechless I had no idea of what the hell Auntie was talking about. All I remember is my mama telling me since I was little that auntie and her girls thought they were better than us. Hood bougie is what she called them. Every time I would bring them up she would tell me how they were only taking pity on me. It was always about them thinking they were more special than us.

"Mama?" I asked looking at her.

"This ain't about us," Mama responded.

"It's history repeating itself can't you see that?" Auntie asked then she turned to look at me. "Rocco, your mama has manipulated you all your life because of some dick she never got,"

"You stupid bitch," My mama said. She started heading toward Auntie Renee. I grabbed her arm because all this is not what we were here for. Whatever issues they had they were gonna have to talk about at another time.

"No, this shit ain't what we're here for. Paradise call that nigga and get him over here or I'm gonna hurt you. That nigga can't mean that much to you," I told her.

"I'm not calling no damn body. Do whatever the fuck it is that you came to do, cousin," she said with a smart ass tone.

"You would get shot to save a nigga that don't love you. Tell me you ain't that stupid," I told her.

"It doesn't matter if he doesn't love me. I knew the situation when we started what we have. It didn't stop me from loving him though. Yes, I am that stupid. That man has saved my life more times than I care to remember I owe my life to him. He saved me from the shooting in the mall when he didn't have to and from getting raped by your bogus ass friend Alpha," she told me.

"You were in the mall that day?" I asked her with a shocked look.

"You were the one trying to kill him at the mall?" She asked looking like she already knew the answer.

"Yeah his punk ass was the one," Chaos answered as he walked in the house.

"Looks like the nigga came on his own," I said with a smile on my face.

"What are you doing here?" Paradise asked him.

"I got a phone call. Rocco you wanna do this here in front of ya family? Should've known your ass was gonna make a bitch ass move soon. You've been too quiet, I know you know I've been looking for you. Paradise or her mom don't have shit to do with none of this bullshit," he said.

He started walking up to me and, I did the same to him.

"I can't believe you brought this shit to my house," Auntie said to my mama.

"How you bring them into some shit you started? I ain't have no beef with you back then but, I damn sure do now," Chaos said with nothing but, hate in his eyes for me.

Up until now I never realized how much I hated him as well. He was right though, he didn't do anything to me for us to come to this point I just didn't like him. Chaos was always walking around like he was that nigga. There wasn't a female around that wouldn't gladly cheat on her nigga just to see this niggas dick. It was sickening to my stomach how everyone was on his dick. All of this started because I was trying to show the nigga that was with me that he was just a nigga like the rest of us. They were all talking about him like he was some God out here or something. He wasn't shit and everyone needed to see that. I didn't plan on getting my ass beat. The guys I was with were supposed to jump in and help at least. When they didn't, I had to come back with something else. That's what made me shoot at him in the mall that day. I tried to ease the knife out of the back of my jeans but, I guess Paradise saw the knife because by the time I tried to stab Chaos she was in the way. I didn't realize she was the one I stabbed until he dropped to his knees pleading with her to open her eyes.

"Paradise, why did you do that? I told you I was gonna protect you not the other way around. Come on babygirl open your eyes for me," he begged her. He took off the shirt that he had on and pressed it on her wound.

"Rocco, get out of here!" My mama yelled.

That was the last thing I remember before I took off running out of the house.

To be continued

ALSO BY TOY

Toxin always admired the marriages of his fellow brothers; however he felt it was never meant for him. The one time he threw caution to the wind, it smacked him in the face like a wind storm in Chicago. Toxin's ex (Shonda) left gifts of hurt, deceit and disloyalty on his heart and her last gift leaves Toxin speechless. Toxin has been living the bachelor life since; promising himself to never give a woman his heart again. However, somethings are out of his control, when God blesses him with a gift. Ivy Dixin has always been a no-nonsense type of woman. A man wasn't a priority in her life. Her business was her husband, baby and best friend. She made her own money as a financial advisor to the rich. Ivy loved the power and control she possessed; she handled the legacies of her clients in her hand; making life changing decisions with a click of her fingers. Meeting Toxin takes Ivy out of her element. Is Ivy open to giving the power of her heart to Toxin? Is Toxin willing to accept the gift of Love?

ALSO BY TOY

If Gertie Grand had one wish for this holiday season it would be for her 3 sons to find true love and to finally become a grandmother. After the death of her husband; Malcom, Melvin and Maceo did all they could to feel the void in Gertie's life, her wish was their command. So why is it so hard for them to grant her the one wish that she desperately longs for? Malcolm Grand has loved and lost love tragically. He has closed himself off from love for years; however he is willing to go to extreme measures to grant his mother the one wish of being able to enjoy a grandchild. Malcolm had a plan to ensure this for Gertie, but what he did not expect was for this plan to begin to break down the walls around his heart. Melvin Grand has loved his best friend Courtney since high-school. They kept their bestie relationship going until Melvin realized that his playboy ways were getting redundant; he knew that Courtney held the key to his heart. However Courtney never wanted to sacrifice their friendship for a broken relationship and heart. If they had one wish Melvin would be able to commit totally Courtney and give his heart what it has been yearning for all these years. Maceo Grand never thought that taking his mother shopping one day will have him run into a blast from his past. A past that could become a beautiful present. However, Nicole came with baggage, a broken heart, a crazy ex and twin boys. Family is not always blood relations and Gertie couldn't be happier to except Nicole's boys as her grandchildren. Where does that leave Maceo and Nichole though. Only if Gertie had one wish, they would become a beautiful love story. When it's a Grand Holiday anything is capable of happening, find out if Gertie gets her one wish for the holidays.

CPSIA information can be obtained
at www.ICGtesting.com
Printed in the USA
LVHW111743120220
646719LV00006B/1111